YASUKE

DEAD MAN WALKING

Braxton A. Cosby

YASUKE

DEAD MAN WALKING

Braxton A. Cosby

YASUKE: DEAD MAN WALKING - BOOK 1

Published by Cosby Media Productions, Inc.
Atlanta, Georgia

www.cosbymediaproductions.com

Cover Art Design: Braxton A. Cosby
Cover art: Cosby Media Productions, Inc.

First Edition, February 2026

Published in the United States of America

Editor: CMP
ISBN: 979-8-89965-078-9

Contact Information: info@cosbymediaproductions.com

PRAISE FOR YASUKE

OUR VERDICT; GET IT – *"An African man trains to be a samurai in Cosby's historical novel…the story is compelling, with some violence and much court intrigue. The author includes a lot of great detail; some of the descriptions of Japan, especially of the natural features, are quite beautiful… and the battle scenes are tightly composed and suspenseful… An engaging historical epic."* – **KIRKUS REVIEW**

5 STARS – *"I was pulled into the grounded emotional beats first rather than the sword clashes…The writing keeps these moments vivid without slowing things down…The fantasy elements appear with restraint at first, which I liked, because it keeps the genre grounded in history while still promising something larger…The action scenes hit hard, while the emotional ones are slow and thoughtful…If you enjoy tales of rising power, morally complex leaders, richly built worlds, and characters shaped by both tenderness and violence, this book will speak to you."* – **LITERARY TITAN**

5 STARS – *"In **Yasuke: Dead Man Walking**, Braxton Cosby merges history and adventure beautifully… The book blends major battles and emotional moments in a way that pulls the reader in… Themes of bravery and loyalty run through the narrative… personal stories and historical events are intertwined, making history feel alive. Anyone who likes historical adventures with strong characters and a mix of action and heart will enjoy this book. Very highly recommended."* – **DAVID JAGGART for READERS' FAVORITE**

DEDICATION

This book is dedicated to the memory of my father, Robert Leroy Cosby. For through his actions, he taught me the valuable lesson that men are not expected to be perfect, but they should be good.

TABLE OF CONTENTS

Chapter 1: The Owl 1
Chapter 2: The Phoenix 14
Chapter 3: The Tiger 22
Chapter 4: The Hachiko 31
Chapter 5: The Japa 43
Chapter 6: The Settei 56
Chapter 7: The Bicha 64
Chapter 8: The Junbi 78
Chapter 9: The Mitingu 91
Chapter 10: The Mwali 105
Chapter 11: The Shokubai 120
Chapter 12: The Wariat 132
Chapter 13: The Dhen 141
Chapter 14: The Obake 151
Chapter 15: The Ya 162
Chapter 16: The Saikuo 169
Chapter 17: The Senso 178
Chapter 18: The Alɔŋ 196
Chapter 19: The Muhon 207
Chapter 20: The Athɔ̈m 221
EPILOGUE 231
ABOUT THE AUTHOR 234
OTHER OFFERINGS FROM THE YASUKE STORY 235

Chapter 1: The Owl

Year 1549

The smoke from burning incense mingled with the heavy scent of sake and sweat, creating a haze that seemed to swallow the flickering candlelight whole. In the depths of the Floating Willow, one of Kyoto's most notorious pleasure quarters, the sound of shamisen strings being plucked lazily drifted through the paper-thin walls, accompanied by the soft giggles of courtesans and the drunken laughter of their patrons.

Oda Nobunaga lay sprawled across silk cushions, his kimono disheveled and hanging loosely from his broad shoulders. At seventeen, he possessed the lean, predatory build of a born warrior, but tonight those muscles were slack with drink and indulgence. His dark hair, usually tied back in the traditional topknot befitting his station, had come undone and fell in unruly waves around his face. Two women flanked him—one tracing lazy circles on his chest while the other poured sake into his already overflowing cup.

"Another toast!" Nobunaga declared, his voice carrying the boisterous confidence that had earned him the whispered title throughout Owari Province: *The Fool of Owari*. His companions, a collection of young lords and merchants' sons seeking favor, raised their cups with bleary-eyed enthusiasm.

"To what shall we drink this time, my lord?" asked Kenji, a portly young man whose father controlled several rice fields along the Kiso River.

Nobunaga's eyes, still sharp despite the alcohol coursing through his veins, glinted with mischief. "To the Gion Matsuri! To another successful festival! And to my dear father, who believes I'm home studying the art of governance!" His laughter was infectious, and soon the entire room erupted in renewed merriment.

The celebration had been building for hours, a continuation of the revelry that had consumed Kyoto during the final day of the Gion Matsuri festival. The Yamaboko Junko procession had wound through the streets that very afternoon, its towering floats and ancient ceremonies drawing thousands of spectators. While his father, Oda Nobuhide, had hosted dignitaries and allies in their family compound with the solemnity expected of a daimyo, Nobunaga had slipped away to find his own version of celebration.

As one of the courtesans began to massage his shoulders, Nobunaga felt the familiar thrill of defiance course through him. Every disapproving glance from his father's retainers, every whispered concern about his "eccentric behavior," only fueled his desire to push boundaries further. They called him a fool, but he knew something they didn't—being underestimated was often the greatest advantage a future leader could possess.

The sake cup slipped from his fingers, clattering to the wooden floor as his eyelids grew heavy. The woman beside him began to hum a soft melody, her voice weaving through his consciousness like a lullaby. Nobunaga felt himself drifting, the voices around him becoming distant echoes.

It was then that the door to their private chamber slid open with such force that it rattled on its tracks.

"Nobunaga-sama."

The voice cut through the haze like a blade through silk. Every person in the room froze, their sake cups suspended midway to their lips, their laughter dying in their throats. The courtesans scrambled to cover themselves, while Nobunaga's companions suddenly found great interest in the patterns on the floor mats.

Standing in the doorway was Ostrimyo, his father's most trusted retainer and the one man in all of Owari Province who could strike fear into Nobunaga's heart without drawing a sword. Despite his advanced years, the old samurai commanded the room with his presence. His long, silver beard was meticulously maintained, and his eyes—those ancient, wise eyes that seemed to see through every deception—held a mixture of disappointment and barely controlled anger. Even bent with age, his frame still suggested the formidable warrior he had once been, the man who had served three generations of the Oda clan.

"Ostrimyo-san," Nobunaga managed, struggling to sit upright. The sake that had felt so pleasant moments before now churned uneasily in his stomach. "How did you—"

"Find you?" The old man's voice carried the weight of decades of service and disappointment. "I have been searching since midnight, my lord. Your father hosted the ceremonial dinner for the Yamabuko Junko, and you were expected to be present. When you failed to appear..." He let the sentence hang in the air like an unsheathed blade.

Nobunaga waved dismissively, though the gesture lacked his usual confidence. "The old men can discuss politics and alliances without me. I was celebrating the festival in my own way." He gestured to his companions, who had begun to edge toward the door. "Isn't that what festivals are for?"

Ostrimyo's gaze swept over the scene—the scattered sake cups, the disheveled clothing, the obvious debauchery—and his jaw tightened. "Perhaps you are right, young master. But celebrations end, and responsibilities remain." He stepped fully into the room, and despite his age, every person present could sense the coiled power that still resided in his weathered frame. "Get dressed. We return home immediately."

"But the night is still young," Nobunaga protested, though even he could hear the weakness in his own voice. Something in Ostrimyo's demeanor suggested this was not merely about his absence from the dinner.

"The night has been far too long already." The old retainer's voice carried a gravitas that made Nobunaga's friends shuffle nervously. "There are matters that require your immediate attention."

As Nobunaga reluctantly began to gather his clothes, one of the courtesans whispered something in his ear that made him laugh. But when he looked up, Ostrimyo's expression had not changed, and the laughter died in his throat.

The journey back to the Oda compound passed in tense silence. Nobunaga, still swaying slightly from the effects of the sake, rode his mare with less than his usual grace, while Ostrimyo maintained a pace that spoke of urgency. The streets of Kyoto were mostly empty now, save for the occasional group of festival-goers making their way home or merchants preparing for the early morning markets.

When they finally reached the family compound, Ostrimyo led him not to his chambers, but to a smaller building where the servants maintained the bathing facilities. Two elderly women waited there, their faces respectfully downcast, beside a large in-ground bathing pool that had been filled with heated water.

"What is this?" Nobunaga asked, though part of him already understood.

"You will bathe and make yourself presentable," Ostrimyo said, his tone brooking no argument. "And while you do, I will tell you why I spent half the night searching the pleasure quarters of Kyoto for you."

The warm water felt good against Nobunaga's skin as the two women, with practiced efficiency, began to wash away the evidence of his evening's indulgences. But as Ostrimyo began to speak, the pleasant warmth seemed to drain away, replaced by a cold that had nothing to do with the temperature of the bath.

"Your friend, Hinata Osi," Ostrimyo began, and Nobunaga's head snapped up sharply. Hinata had been his closest companion since childhood, the one person who could match his appetite for mischief and adventure. "He was found this morning in his family's garden."

"Found?" Nobunaga's voice came out as barely more than a whisper.

"Dead, my lord. The physician believes it was alcohol poisoning. He had been drinking alone after the festival ended, celebrating what he called his last night of freedom before his arranged marriage next month." Ostrimyo's voice softened slightly, showing the first crack in his stern demeanor. "His servants found him at dawn."

The words hit Nobunaga like a physical blow. He had shared countless adventures with Hinata, had planned to stand beside him at his wedding, had imagined decades of friendship stretching ahead of them. Now, in an instant, all of that was gone. The sake that had brought such joy hours earlier had become an instrument of death.

As the servants continued their work, washing his hair and scrubbing his skin, Nobunaga felt something shift inside him. The carefree abandon that had defined his evening now seemed not just foolish, but almost grotesque. While he had been laughing in the arms of courtesans, his dearest friend had been dying alone.

"I should have been there," he said, his voice barely audible over the gentle splashing of water.

"Where?" Ostrimyo asked. "At his side, drinking yourself into the same grave? Or here, learning the skills you will need to lead when your father's time comes?"

The old retainer moved closer to the edge of the pool, his reflection wavering in the disturbed water. "Nobunaga-sama, I have served your family for over forty years. I watched your grandfather build the foundation of Oda power, and I have watched your father expand it. But power built on indulgence and frivolity is like a castle built on sand—impressive to look at, but doomed to collapse at the first strong wind."

"I know my responsibilities," Nobunaga said, though the words lacked conviction.

"Do you?" Ostrimyo's eyes blazed with an intensity that made Nobunaga recoil slightly. "You are the heir to one of the most important domains in central Japan. The Sengoku period has turned our land into a battlefield where only the strongest and wisest survive. Your father has spent decades navigating these treacherous waters, building alliances, crushing enemies, all to secure a future for the Oda clan. And what do you do with this legacy? You squander your nights in pleasure quarters, earning yourself a reputation as a fool."

The harsh words stung, but Nobunaga found he could not argue with them. As the servants helped him from the bath and began to dry him with soft cloths, he felt exposed in more ways than one.

"One day you may inherit this domain," Ostrimyo continued, his voice dropping to a whisper that somehow carried more weight than any shout. "And if you do, you could squander it all away with your frivolous behavior. The other daimyo are watching, waiting for any sign of weakness. Your uncle Nobuyuki already whispers to anyone who will listen that he would be a more suitable heir. Your own retainers begin to doubt your fitness to lead."

Nobunaga looked up sharply at this. He had suspected his uncle's ambitions, but hearing it stated so bluntly was like a knife to the chest.

"What would you have me do?" he asked, genuine uncertainty creeping into his voice for the first time.

Ostrimyo knelt beside him as the servants finished their work and retreated to a respectful distance. When he spoke, his voice carried not just authority, but something approaching paternal concern.

"The only way to be a king, Nobunaga-sama, is to be a king in all that you do. Every action, every word, every moment of your life must reflect the weight of the responsibility you will one day carry. Your enemies will not wait for you to mature. They will not give you time to learn through failure. They will strike at the first sign of weakness, and if you are not ready..." He let the implication hang in the air.

As they made their way back to Nobunaga's chambers, the young lord found his mind clearer than it had been in months. Hinata's death had shaken something loose in him, some vital understanding that had been buried under layers of wine and indulgence. The morning sun was beginning to creep over the horizon, painting the compound in shades of gold and orange, and for the first time in recent memory, Nobunaga found himself eager to see what the dawn would bring.

One Year Later

The hill overlooking the Oda domain had become Nobunaga's sanctuary, a place where the weight of expectations and the press of daily responsibilities could not reach him. In the soft light of dawn, with mist still clinging to the valleys below, he knelt across from his private tutor, Chi Handiomidon, a scholarly man whose weathered face spoke of decades spent in study and contemplation.

"Tell me again about the Sengoku period," Nobunaga said, his voice carrying none of the casual indifference that had once characterized his approach to learning. The transformation in the young lord over the past year had been remarkable—where once he had struggled to sit still for even brief lessons, he now absorbed knowledge with the intensity of a man dying of thirst.

Chi Handiomidon smiled, recognizing the hunger in his student's eyes. "The Warring States period began nearly a century ago, when the Ashikaga shogunate lost its ability to control the provinces. What followed was the fracturing of Japan into dozens of independent domains, each ruled by a daimyo who recognizes no authority but his own."

Nobunaga nodded, his gaze sweeping over the landscape below. From this vantage point, he could see the borders of his father's domain stretching to meet those of their neighbors—some allies, some enemies, all potential threats.

"And the key to survival in such times?" Nobunaga asked, though he suspected he already knew the answer.

"Adaptation," Chi Handiomidon replied without hesitation. "The old ways of honor and rigid loyalty are luxuries we can no longer afford. In the Sengoku period, the daimyo who survives is the one who can form complex alliances, who understands that today's enemy may be tomorrow's most valuable ally. Marriages of convenience, temporary truces, shifting loyalties—these are the tools of statecraft in our age."

The lesson continued as the sun climbed higher, but Nobunaga found his attention divided. Part of him absorbed every word his tutor spoke, filing away details about trade routes and military formations, alliance networks and succession disputes. But another part of his mind was already racing ahead, imagining how he might apply these lessons, how he might not just survive in this fractured world, but master it.

When the lesson concluded, Nobunaga made his way down the hill toward his home and glanced over at the Arena of Kenka, the open-air dojo that occupied a central position in the family compound. He sighed, knowing soon that another kind of education awaited him.

As he rose the next morning, he gathered his things and made his way over to the Arena of Kenka. When he arrived, The Akarui was already waiting, his wooden practice sword resting easily in his hands. The man's nickname, meaning "bright light," perfectly captured his personality—he approached combat with an almost joyful intensity, finding genuine pleasure in the art of warfare. Despite being well into his middle years, he moved with the fluid grace of a master warrior, and in all the years Nobunaga had trained under him, the young lord had never managed to achieve victory.

Today felt different, though. As Nobunaga picked up his own wooden sword and settled into his fighting stance, he could sense something had changed in the balance between them. Perhaps it was the year of dedicated training, the countless hours spent perfecting his technique and building his endurance. Or perhaps it was something deeper—the fundamental shift in his approach to everything since Hinata's death and Ostrimyo's harsh words.

"Are you ready, young master?" The Akarui asked, his smile carrying both warmth and challenge.

Instead of answering with words, Nobunaga launched himself forward. The wooden swords met with a sharp crack that echoed off the surrounding buildings, and immediately both men knew this would be unlike their previous encounters. Where once Nobunaga had relied primarily on strength and aggression, now his attacks showed patience and calculation. He pressed when he sensed weakness, withdrew when he faced solid defense, and gradually began to exploit the older man's greatest vulnerability—his age.

The battle stretched on far longer than any they had fought before. Both men were soon streaming with sweat, their breathing labored, their movements beginning to slow. But where The Akarui's endurance flagged, Nobunaga seemed to find new reserves of energy. His year of disciplined training, of early mornings and rigorous exercise, now paid dividends that had nothing to do with technique and everything to do with raw physical conditioning.

Finally, in a moment that seemed to stretch endlessly, Nobunaga saw his opening. The Akarui's guard dropped slightly as fatigue took its toll, and Nobunaga struck with lightning precision, his wooden blade stopping just short of his opponent's throat.

For a long moment, both men stood frozen in tableau. Then The Akarui stepped back and formally bowed, yielding victory to his student for the first time in their years of training together.

"Well fought, Nobunaga-sama," The Akarui said, and there was genuine pride in his voice. "You have finally learned the most important lesson of combat—that victory often goes not to the most skilled, but to the most prepared."

From the edge of the training ground, slow applause drew their attention. Ostrimyo stood watching, his expression unreadable. As he approached the two fighters, Nobunaga felt a familiar tension—would the old retainer find some fault with even this achievement?

"You have improved remarkably this past year," Ostrimyo said, and his tone carried an approval that Nobunaga had rarely heard directed at him. "Your technique has sharpened, your endurance has grown, and most importantly, your discipline has matured. You are becoming more and more like your father. When the time comes, you will be ready for succession."

The words should have filled Nobunaga with pride, but instead they carried a strange weight of premonition. Something in Ostrimyo's tone suggested that "when the time comes" might be sooner than anyone expected.

1551

The funeral of Oda Nobuhide was a spectacle that would be remembered for generations. Daimyo from across central Japan came to pay their respects to the man who had been both ally and enemy, whose political acumen and military prowess had made him one of the most influential figures of his generation. The ceremony itself lasted three days, with Buddhist monks chanting sutras while incense smoke rose like prayers toward the heavens.

Nobunaga knelt at the center of it all, formally dressed in the white robes of mourning, his face a mask of controlled grief. At eighteen, he now possessed the lean, hard look of a seasoned warrior, but in this moment, watching his father's body prepared for its final journey, he looked younger than his years.

The tears came despite his efforts to maintain composure. They had not been close in recent years—his father's disappointment in his early behavior had created a distance that was only beginning to heal when illness struck. But Nobuhide had been the foundation upon which Nobunaga's entire world rested, and now that foundation was gone.

His mother, Dota Gozen, knelt beside him, her own grief carefully controlled. She had been instrumental in securing Nobunaga's position as heir, arguing successfully against those who favored his older brother or his uncle. Now, as she watched her son struggle with the weight of sudden responsibility, she wondered if she had done him any favors.

Days later, the coronation ceremony that would formally install Nobunaga as the new lord of the Oda domain was held in the main hall of the family compound. Representatives from allied domains attended, along with the senior retainers and military commanders who would now serve under his leadership.

But as Nobunaga knelt before the ancestral tablets and prepared to accept the formal symbols of his authority, he became aware of a disturbance behind him. Turning slightly, he saw something that cut deeper than any sword stroke ever could.

His uncle, Oda Nobuyuki, was rising from his position among the assembled family members. Behind him, Nobunaga's two cousins were doing the same. Even his own older brother, whose support he had taken for granted, stood and turned his back to the ceremony.

One by one, they filed out of the hall in a deliberate display of rejection to the now seventeen-year-old prodigy. The message was clear—they did not recognize his authority, did not accept his right to lead the clan. The political implications were staggering, but the personal betrayal cut even deeper.

As the heavy doors closed behind his departing relatives, Nobunaga felt the full weight of his isolation settle upon him. The allies who remained were outnumbered by those who had left, and every person present understood that the Oda clan was now divided against itself.

But in that moment of abandonment, something crystallized in Nobunaga's mind. The lessons of the past year—about adaptation, about complex alliances, about the brutal realities of the Sengoku period—suddenly took on new urgency. His enemies were not distant daimyo in far-off provinces. They were sitting at his own dinner table, bearing his own name, plotting his downfall from within his own family.

As he formally accepted the symbols of leadership, Nobunaga made a silent vow. He would not merely survive the treachery that surrounded him—he would master it. The Fool of Owari was dead, buried alongside his father. What rose to take his place would be something far more dangerous: a young lord with nothing left to lose and everything to prove.

The Sengoku period was about to meet its match.

Chapter 2: The Phoenix

Two Weeks Later

The morning mist clung to the rolling hills of Owari Province like the breath of sleeping dragons, dissipating slowly as the sun climbed higher into a sky painted in shades of pearl and gold. Nobunaga walked beside Ostrimyo along a narrow path that wound through terraced rice fields, their footsteps creating a rhythmic counterpoint to the soft rustle of armed guards who maintained a respectful but vigilant distance.

The young daimyo had changed in the two weeks since his father's funeral and the bitter betrayal of his family. Where once he might have complained about the early hour or the length of their journey, now he moved with the focused intensity of a man who understood that every moment was a lesson in survival. His hand rested casually on the grip of his katana, a gesture that had become as natural as breathing.

"Ostrimyo-san," Nobunaga said, breaking the comfortable silence that had settled between them. "I have been thinking about our conversation regarding my new responsibilities as daimyo. There is something I wish to discuss with you."

The old retainer glanced at his young lord, noting the serious tone. "Of course, Nobunaga-sama. What weighs on your mind?"

"Your role in all of this. You served my father faithfully for decades, guided him through countless challenges. Now you do the same for me, but I realize we have never formally defined what this relationship means." Nobunaga paused in his walking, turning to face Ostrimyo directly. "I want to create a new position for you. You will be my Wing—my most trusted advisor, the extension of my will when I cannot be present, the one who guards not just my body but my very soul."

Ostrimyo's weathered face showed surprise, then deep emotion. In all his years of service, no Oda lord had ever offered him such recognition, such trust. "My lord, I am honored beyond words. To serve as your Wing would be the greatest privilege of my life."

They resumed their walk, but something fundamental had shifted between them. This was no longer simply a retainer serving his master—this was a partnership forged in the crucible of political necessity and mutual respect.

"Now then," Ostrimyo said, his voice carrying new authority in his role as Wing. "Let us speak of what it truly means to be a daimyo. You rule this land not as an independent king, but as a vassal to the Shogun, who serves as military dictator under the Emperor. This chain of loyalty is what maintains order in our fractured nation."

Nobunaga nodded, but his eyes held a glint that Ostrimyo had learned to recognize—the look of a young man whose ambitions stretched far beyond the boundaries others had set for him.

"But tell me, Ostrimyo-san," Nobunaga said carefully, "is it possible for a daimyo to rise beyond his station? Could one perhaps catch the eye of the Shogun, prove himself worthy of greater responsibility?"

"You speak of becoming Shogun yourself," Ostrimyo observed, and there was no judgment in his voice, only curiosity.

"And if I did? If I dared to dream of wielding that kind of power—not just over Owari, but over all of Japan?"

Ostrimyo chuckled, but it was not the laughter of mockery. Rather, it carried the warm approval of a teacher whose student had just asked exactly the right question. "My young lord, ambition is like fire—it can warm a house or burn it to the ground, depending on how skillfully it is controlled. Yes, it is possible for a daimyo to rise. History has shown us examples of men who seized power through military might and political cunning. But," he held up a weathered finger, "you have a very long way to go before such dreams become possibilities."

They crested a small hill, and Ostrimyo gestured toward the valley below where farmers worked their fields and smoke rose from village hearths. "First, you must build your strength here, in your own domain. You must train powerful samurai to serve as your personal guard, men whose loyalty to you transcends their loyalty to clan or tradition. If you can forge a truly formidable army, one that catches the attention of the Shogun like a fox catches a rodent, then perhaps you might be taken under his wing. From there..." He shrugged eloquently.

"From there, anything becomes possible," Nobunaga finished, his voice carrying a quiet intensity that made even the guards glance in his direction.

"But before you can conquer Japan," Ostrimyo continued with a slight smile, "you must secure your own house. And that means taking a bride. A daimyo without an heir is a daimyo whose domain will not survive him."

Nobunaga's expression darkened slightly. "You speak of marriage as if it were another military alliance. Where is the honor in that? And what role could a woman possibly play in ruling? She would be expected to obey, to follow, to bear children. How could such a person be of any use in governance?"

Ostrimyo stopped walking entirely, his expression growing serious. "Ah, my lord, here is where your youth shows most clearly. Yes, you could rule your wife with an iron fist, demand absolute obedience, treat her as nothing more than a vessel for your heirs. But such an approach would waste one of your most valuable potential assets."

"How so?"

"Consider this wisdom carefully: many a ruler has met his demise by a blade in the dark, struck down by a spouse grown tired of tyranny and humiliation. But more than that—a good wife sees things from a softer, wider gaze than we warriors often possess. She can be your greatest asset when dealing with the cries of the people, when understanding the currents of emotion that flow beneath the surface of politics. Rule her with a soft but firm grasp, and she becomes your partner. Rule her with cruelty, and she becomes your enemy."

Nobunaga absorbed this in thoughtful silence as they continued their journey. The wisdom made sense, though it challenged everything he had assumed about marriage and power. As they walked, he found himself wondering what kind of woman could serve as such a partner, and whether he would recognize her when the time came.

Days Later

The lake stretched before them like a mirror of polished bronze, its surface broken only by the occasional ripple as fish rose to feed on insects. Ancient pines lined the shore, their gnarled branches reaching toward a sky painted in the soft hues of late afternoon. It was here, in this place of natural beauty and tranquility, that Ostrimyo had chosen to continue Nobunaga's education in the art of rulership.

Nobunaga moved through the water with powerful, measured strokes, his swimming both exercise and meditation. The lake was deep enough that he could not touch bottom, forcing him to rely entirely on his own strength and endurance—a lesson that extended far beyond the physical realm.

From the shore, Ostrimyo's voice carried clearly across the water, his words punctuated by the gentle lapping of waves against the rocky bank. "To understand your role as daimyo, you must first understand the world you inhabit, my lord. Japan is built upon a rigid hierarchy that has maintained order for centuries."

Nobunaga executed a perfect turn and began swimming back toward shore, his breathing controlled despite the exertion. "Tell me about this hierarchy," he called out between strokes.

"At the top stand the samurai—the warrior class to which you belong. We are the sword arm of society, responsible for maintaining order and defending the realm. Below us come the farmers, who feed the nation and whose labors support everything else. Then the artisans, who create the tools and beauty that make civilization possible. Finally, at the bottom, the merchants—necessary but often despised because they produce nothing, merely moving goods from place to place."

"And where do the daimyo fit in this structure?" Nobunaga asked as he reached the shallows and began wading toward shore.

"We are samurai elevated by birth and achievement to rule over specific domains. Our authority within our lands is near-absolute, but we remain bound by duty to those above us in the hierarchy."

As Nobunaga emerged from the lake, water streaming from his lean frame, the transformation of the past months was clearly visible. His body had hardened into that of a true warrior—lean but powerful muscles moving beneath skin that spoke of countless hours of training and discipline. The soft indulgence of his youth had been burned away, replaced by the steel-hard physique of a man prepared for the brutal realities of leadership.

The house maids who had been waiting respectfully in the shade of the pine trees moved forward with practiced efficiency, but without the hurried nervousness that had once characterized their service. Nobunaga's newfound focus and maturity had earned the respect of even the humblest servants. As they draped him in a light cotton robe and began the process of drying him off, he remained entirely focused on Ostrimyo's words, unbothered by his nakedness or the attention of the servants.

"You mentioned that most Japanese have never encountered foreigners," Nobunaga said as the maids worked. "But I have heard stories of Portuguese and Spanish visitors in certain ports."

"Indeed," Ostrimyo confirmed. "There are limited numbers of missionaries and traders who have been granted permission to operate in specific locations. But these contacts are carefully controlled. Most of our people have never laid eyes on anyone from beyond our shores, particularly anyone from Africa. The isolation has served us well in some ways, preserving our culture and independence. But it also means we know little of the wider world."

Once properly dressed, Nobunaga settled onto a flat stone near the water's edge, his expression growing more serious. "Ostrimyo-san, I must confess something that has been weighing heavily on my heart. The disappearance of my family since my coronation... it saddens me more than I expected."

The old retainer's expression softened with understanding. "You speak of your brother, your uncle Nobuyuki, and your cousins Nobumasa and Nobukatsu."

"Yes. I had hoped that time might heal the rift between us, that they might come to accept my position and return to the family. Instead, they seem to have vanished entirely from Owari. I worry that my ascension has cost me the only family I have left."

Ostrimyo was quiet for a long moment, watching the play of light on the lake's surface. When he spoke, his voice carried the weight of hard-earned wisdom. "My lord, to be a good ruler, you may be forced to make difficult decisions about relationships that no longer serve your best interests. Think of it like pruning a Black Pine—the gardener must clip away certain leaves and branches so that nourishment can flow more effectively to the trunk, making the entire tree stronger."

"But surely family is different," Nobunaga protested. "My family would never truly wish me harm, would they?"

"As daimyo, you must always remain alert to those closest to you," Ostrimyo said, his tone growing grave. "Jealousy and envy are potent emotional drugs that can cut deeper into the soul than any blade ever forged. When anyone in your circle—friends, servants, military commanders, family members, even trusted companions—becomes intoxicated with either of these emotions, your bond with them is officially broken. They cease to be allies and become opposition, regardless of the blood you share."

The words hit Nobunaga like physical blows. "Do you foresee such betrayals in my future?"

Ostrimyo's eyes met his directly, and in them Nobunaga saw not cruelty, but the profound sadness of a man who had witnessed too much of human nature's darker aspects. "It is inevitable, my lord. Your father faced many such choices during his time as daimyo. He learned, as you must learn, that leadership sometimes requires cutting away even that which we love most dearly. The question is not whether such moments will come, but whether you will have the strength to act when they do."

As the sun began to set over the lake, painting the water in shades of gold and crimson, Nobunaga felt another piece of his childhood innocence fall away. The world was revealing itself to be far more complex and dangerous than he had ever imagined, a place where love and loyalty could transform into weapons as deadly as any sword.

But he was no longer the frightened boy who had wept at his father's funeral. He was becoming something harder, something more dangerous—a leader who understood that survival required not just strength and cunning, but the willingness to sacrifice anything and anyone for the greater good of his domain and his ambitions.

The phoenix was beginning to spread its wings, and when it finally took flight, all of Japan would feel the wind from its passage.

Chapter 3: The Tiger

One Month Later

The mountain path wound through ancient cedars whose towering trunks blocked out most of the afternoon sun, creating a cathedral of shadows and filtered light. Nobunaga rode at the head of his small retinue, his posture relaxed despite the ten armed samurai who flanked him on either side. The meeting with the Azai clan leader had gone better than expected—their alliance was now formally sealed, adding another crucial piece to the complex puzzle of regional politics.

"The Azai understand the value of aligning themselves with strength," Ostrimyo observed, his mare keeping pace beside Nobunaga's stallion. As his Wing, the old retainer had been present for every moment of the negotiations, his counsel proving invaluable in navigating the delicate balance between respect and authority.

"Azai Hisamasa is pragmatic," Nobunaga agreed. "He sees which way the wind is blowing in Owari Province. Better to be my ally than my enemy." There was a hardness in his voice that would have been alien to the pleasure-seeking youth of two years past. Leadership had carved away everything soft in him, leaving behind something sharper, more dangerous.

The attack came without warning.

Arrows whistled from the dense undergrowth on both sides of the path, and Nobunaga's horse reared as a shaft buried itself in the animal's neck. Time seemed to slow as he threw himself from the saddle, his katana singing from its scabbard even before his feet touched the ground.

"Ambush!" Ostrimyo's voice cut through the chaos as more arrows filled the air. "Form up! Protect the lord!"

But there was no time to form any proper defense. Men emerged from the forest like demons materializing from shadow—twenty of them, their faces hidden behind masks but their intent unmistakably lethal. At their head stood three figures whose postures Nobunaga recognized with a shock that cut deeper than any blade.

His uncle, Oda Nobuyuki. His cousins, Nobumasa and Nobukatsu.

"Uncle," Nobunaga said, his voice carrying across the mountainside with deadly calm. "I had wondered where you had gone."

"You wondered?" Nobuyuki's voice dripped with contempt as he drew his sword. "Did you wonder if we would simply accept your theft of what rightfully belongs to our family? Did you think we would bow before a boy who earned his position through his mother's manipulation rather than his own merit?"

Around them, the battle had already begun in earnest. Nobunaga's samurai, caught off guard by the sudden assault, fought with desperate courage against overwhelming odds. The ring of steel on steel echoed through the forest, punctuated by cries of pain and the wet sound of blades finding flesh.

"You could have been my allies," Nobunaga said, circling slowly as his uncle advanced. "You could have shared in the glory I intend to build. Instead, you chose treachery."

"We choose justice," Nobukatsu snarled, raising his own weapon. "The Oda clan deserves better than a pretender who—"

His words ended in a gurgle as Nobunaga moved with lightning speed, covering the distance between them in two fluid steps. His katana swept in a perfect arc, opening his cousin's throat in a spray of crimson. The young man's eyes widened in shock before the light faded from them entirely.

"One," Nobunaga said quietly, his blade already moving to parry a strike from Nobumasa.

The second cousin proved more skilled than his brother, his swordwork bearing the mark of years of dedicated training. But Nobunaga had been forged in a different kind of crucible—the desperate school of survival where hesitation meant death. Their blades met in a series of lightning exchanges, sparks flying as steel scraped against steel.

From the corner of his eye, Nobunaga saw Ostrimyo engaged with two attackers, the old warrior's experience allowing him to hold his own despite the numerical disadvantage. But then a third man emerged from behind a tree, his sword aimed directly at Ostrimyo's blind spot.

"Wing!" Nobunaga shouted, but it was too late.

The blade caught Ostrimyo across the face, laying open the flesh from temple to jaw. The old retainer stumbled backward, blood streaming from the wounds, his hands clutching at his eyes as he cried out in pain and rage.

Something primal and terrible awakened in Nobunaga at that moment. The careful control he had cultivated over the past two years shattered like thin ice, replaced by a fury so pure and focused that it seemed to burn the very air around him.

He killed Nobumasa with a thrust that pierced his cousin's heart, then spun to face the man who had wounded Ostrimyo. That samurai died with his own blade buried in his skull. Another fell with his spine severed. A fourth lost his head to a cut so clean it took a moment for the body to realize it was dead.

"Five," Nobunaga whispered, his voice carrying an inhuman quality that made even his own men step back in awe and terror.

The remaining attackers, seeing their advantage evaporate under the fury of his assault, began to retreat. Nobuyuki, bleeding from a dozen minor wounds, backed toward the forest edge.

"This isn't over, nephew," he called out, his voice shaking with equal parts rage and fear. "I am the rightful heir. I will—"

"You will run," Nobunaga said, advancing slowly. Around them, the mountainside had grown eerily quiet except for the moans of the wounded and dying. Of his ten samurai, only two remained standing, both bearing injuries that would mark them for life. "You will flee like the coward you are, and you will remember this day. Remember that when you chose to spill Oda blood, you forfeited any claim to mercy."

His uncle disappeared into the forest, leaving behind a battlefield littered with the dead and dying. Nobunaga knelt beside Ostrimyo, his hands gentle as he examined the terrible wounds that had destroyed the old man's eyes.

"Can you see?" he asked, though he already knew the answer.

"Darkness," Ostrimyo whispered, his voice thick with pain. "Complete darkness, my lord."

The journey back to the compound passed in grim silence. Ostrimyo, despite his wounds, insisted on riding rather than being carried, though Nobunaga stayed close beside him every step of the way. The surviving samurai bore their losses with stoic acceptance, but Nobunaga could see the way they looked at him—with a mixture of respect and something approaching fear.

He had killed five men today. The first lives he had ever taken. The blood on his hands felt both foreign and familiar, as if some part of him had always known this moment would come.

They had barely entered the compound when another crisis presented itself. Standing in the main courtyard, surrounded by a handful of loyal retainers, was Nobunaga's brother, Edo Nobunaga. The young man's face was set in lines of grim determination, and when he saw his older brother approach, he stepped forward with the formal bearing of a man about to invoke ancient law.

"Brother," Edo said, his voice carrying clearly across the courtyard. "I challenge you to a Fight of Bushido for the position of rightful heir to the Oda clan."

Nobunaga stopped short, exhaustion and rage warring within him. After the ambush, after seeing Ostrimyo wounded, after the first blood on his hands, this formal challenge felt like the final insult in a day already too full of betrayal.

"You choose this moment?" Nobunaga asked, his voice dangerously quiet. "While our Wing lies wounded, while the blood of our own family stains my blade, you choose this moment to question my authority?"

"I choose the moment when it has become clear that your leadership brings nothing but violence and division to our clan," Edo replied. "Uncle Nobuyuki may have chosen the path of ambush and treachery, but I will face you with honor. Draw your sword, brother."

The courtyard had filled with people—servants, samurai, retainers—all drawn by the formal nature of the challenge. In the code of Bushido, no lord could refuse such a contest without losing face entirely. But as Nobunaga looked at his older brother, he felt something cold and terrible settling in his chest.

"So be it," he said, drawing his katana. The blade still bore traces of blood from the mountainside battle, and in the torchlight, it seemed to glow with an inner fire.

Edo was skilled—perhaps even more technically proficient than Nobunaga in pure swordsmanship. But skill alone was no longer enough. The boy who had once lost consistently to The Akarui was gone, replaced by a man who had learned to fight not for sport or honor, but for survival.

The duel was brief and brutal. Swords collided as sparks ignited with each forceful pass. Both men moved with equal parts elegance and power, making it difficult for either of them to take a strike. After dancing for a longer period that Nobunaga found acceptable, he finally took his chance to strike.

Edo was narrowing his steps as the two brothers kept pace, in an effort do doubt to conserve his energy. Nobunaga doubled down on the same move he used to defeat The Akarui, thrusting forward as quickly as possible beating Edo's parry. The edge of the blade hit it's mark, slicing through a thick layer of skin along Edo's torso, just barely missing a vital organ. Nobunaga continued his assault, forcing Edo on the defense, slowly wearing down any hope of repelling Nobunaga's blade.

Edo's textbook technique finally crumbled under the relentless pressure of Nobunaga's assault. Where his brother sought elegance and form, Nobunaga brought raw, focused violence. The end came when Edo overextended himself in a desperate attempt to break through Nobunaga's guard, leaving himself open to a thrust to the chest, but this time, piercing a lung.

As Edo fell to his knees, blood frothing from his lips, Nobunaga tossed a short wakizashi at his brother's feet. "Complete it," he said, his voice empty of all emotion. "Die with whatever honor you have left."

Edo's hands shook as he picked up the blade, but his eyes never left Nobunaga's face. "I... I thought I was saving our clan," he whispered.

"You were destroying it," Nobunaga replied. "Just as Uncle did. Just as anyone who stands against me will do."

The seppuku was performed with trembling but determined hands. Edo drew the blade across his stomach in the ritual cut, then fell forward onto the longer katana Nobunaga had placed before him. The courtyard watched in absolute silence as the young lord died, his blood pooling on the stones that had witnessed generations of Oda authority.

When it was over, Nobunaga looked around at the assembled crowd. In their faces, he saw shock, fear, and something else—the absolute recognition of his power. "Let this be understood," he said, his voice carrying to every corner of the courtyard. "I am the heir. I am the lord. Any who question this will share the fate of those who have already chosen to stand against me."

Before Dawn

The oil lamp cast dancing shadows on the walls of Ostrimyo's chamber as Nobunaga knelt beside his Wing's bedside. The old retainer's face was swathed in bandages, but blood still seeped through the white cloth, creating dark stains that spoke of wounds that would never fully heal.

"How do you feel?" Nobunaga asked, though the question seemed almost absurd given the circumstances.

"Like an old fool who let his guard down at precisely the wrong moment," Ostrimyo replied, his voice hoarse but steady. "The physicians have confirmed what we both already know. My sight will not return, my lord. I am blind."

The simple statement hit Nobunaga like a physical blow. This man who had served two generations of Oda lords, who had become more than a retainer—almost a father—had been crippled because of the treachery of Nobunaga's own blood.

"I will have my revenge," Nobunaga said, his hands clenching into fists. "Uncle Nobuyuki thinks he can flee into the mountains and escape justice. He is wrong. I will hunt him down. I will make him pay for what he has done to you."

"Revenge will not restore my sight," Ostrimyo said gently. "And the pursuit of vengeance can consume a man's soul if he is not careful."

"I don't care," Nobunaga snarled, rising to pace the small chamber. "It is time for me to show my absolute power. The other factions think they can test me because of my youth. They whisper that I am still a boy playing at being a lord. Today proved them wrong, but it is not enough."

He stopped pacing and turned to face the bandaged figure on the bed. "There are reports of another uprising—the priests at Mount Hiei have been speaking against my authority, claiming that the kami themselves reject my leadership. They call themselves the Feisty Priests, and they seek to turn the people against me."

"My lord," Ostrimyo said, struggling to sit up. "In your current state of mind, you are dangerous to yourself and others. Do not make decisions born of rage and grief."

"My decisions are born of necessity," Nobunaga replied. "I must set an example of my power. Let the surrounding tribes know that I am not a child, that I am the complete authority in Owari Province. No one but the Shogun or the Emperor stands above me."

As he moved toward the door, Ostrimyo's voice followed him, filled with the weight of prophecy and warning. "Remember, my lord—the tiger who tastes blood often finds that it is never enough to satisfy his hunger."

But Nobunaga was already gone, his mind fixed on the dawn that would bring either triumph or disaster.

The sun had not yet broken the horizon when he led his force out of the compound. This time, he brought not just samurai but true warriors—men who had proven themselves in battle, who understood that mercy was a luxury leaders could not afford. As they rode toward Mount Hiei, Nobunaga felt the familiar thrill of impending violence, the intoxicating rush of absolute power about to be unleashed.

The Feisty Priests had made a fatal error in judgment. They had mistaken the young daimyo for the foolish boy he had once been. By the time the sun set again, they would understand the true nature of the man he had become.

And in the aftermath of that understanding, Nobunaga would claim not just their lives, but something far more precious—the legendary sword Kusanagi-no-Tsurugi, the Heavenly Sword of Gathering Clouds, one of the three Imperial Regalia of Japan itself.

The tiger was about to show his claws, and all of Japan would learn to fear the sound of his roar.

Chapter 4: The Hachiko

1579

The storm had been battering the vessel for the last three days, with pestering winds and violent, brief showers that hinted a something more dangerous on the horizon, turning what should have been calm waters into a churning cauldron of foam and fury. Rain lashed against the wooden hull with the persistence of arrows in battle, while waves the size of mountains lifted the ship skyward before hurling it back toward the depths. But today, the sails had been retracted hours ago, leaving only human muscle to fight against the ocean's wrath.

In the belly of the ship, rows of men with varying shades of dark skin bent their backs to the rhythm of survival, their oars cutting through water that seeped constantly through the hull's joints. The air was thick with salt spray, sweat, and the grunts of exertion that marked each stroke. Above them, through the wooden planking, a voice called out with the authority of command.

"Steady men, steady! Keep the rhythm! We ride with the waves, not against them!"

Among the rowers, one figure stood out even in the dim light filtering through the ship's small portholes. Majok's massive frame moved with mechanical precision, his muscles coiling and releasing with each pull of the oar. Water dripped from his hair and shoulders, but his breathing remained controlled, almost meditative. Beside him, a smaller man—lean where Majok was powerful, wiry where Majok was solid—struggled to match the pace.

The smaller man's eyes kept drifting to his rowing partner, taking in the sheer scale of him, the way he seemed to absorb the ship's violent motion and transform it into steady, powerful strokes. Finally, curiosity overcame exhaustion.

"Where are you from?" he gasped between pulls.

"Originally, the Sudan," Majok replied, his voice carrying easily despite the storm's noise.

"No, like recently, now." The man's breathing was labored, but his curiosity was stronger than his fatigue. "You don't look like a slave and you're no sailor."

Majok's rhythm never faltered, but something shifted in his expression—a shadow of memory crossing his features like clouds over the sun. "My roots run deep. Like a tree. And my story is even deeper. Most likely, not worth the time it will take to listen."

"Please share," the man said, managing a weak smile despite their circumstances. "I've got nothing else to do but waste time."

For a moment, Majok considered the request. The storm showed no signs of abating, and there was something in his rowing companion's voice—a genuine hunger for human connection that reminded him of... other times, other places. He pulled once more on his oar, and then began to speak, his voice taking on the rhythm of the waves.

"Very well. But if you're looking for a simple tale, you'll be disappointed."

1568

"I was enslaved as a child," Majok began, his voice steady despite the ship's violent pitching. "Thirteen or fourteen years old, I can't

recall exactly. Memory has a way of protecting us from the worst of our pain by blurring the details that would otherwise destroy us."

The scene shifted in his mind, pulling him back across years and oceans to a time when his world was measured not in nautical miles but in the distance between villages, when his concerns centered not on storms at sea but on whether the rains would come to nourish the crops his people depended upon.

He had been born to the Dinka people, in the vast grasslands that stretched beyond the horizon like a green ocean under African skies. His father had been a warrior, his mother a keeper of seeds—a woman who understood the ancient mysteries of coaxing life from apparently dead earth. From her, young Majok had learned that death and life were not opposites but partners in an eternal dance.

"She taught me to hunt," he said, his oar cutting through the water with renewed purpose. "Not just animals, but knowledge. How to read the signs that told you where water could be found even in the dry season. How to gather roots and berries that could sustain you when game was scarce. But most importantly, she taught me about agriculture—how plants could grow in the absence of obvious sustenance, how something that appeared dead could be brought back to life with patience and understanding."

He remembered kneeling beside her in their family's small plot, his young hands learning to feel the difference between soil that would nurture and soil that would merely hold. She had shown him how to plant seeds not just in earth, but in hope—how to tend something you might not live to harvest, but which would feed your children's children.

"The slave traders came during the harvest season," Majok continued, his voice growing harder. "They knew that was when families would be together, when the men would be in from the ranges and the women and children would be gathered close to home. They surrounded our village before dawn, when the cooking fires were just being lit and the day's work was about to begin."

The memory was fragmented, like pottery shattered by a careless hand. He could recall his mother's scream, the sound of his father's spear striking a raider's shield, the smell of smoke as their hut caught fire. Then running, always running, until calloused hands caught him and the world he had known ceased to exist.

The journey to the coast had taken weeks, chained to dozens of other captured souls, watching some fall by the wayside when their strength failed them. Then the ship—the real slave ship, unlike the vessel that carried him now—where darkness and despair had been the only constants.

"The crossing to India took months," Majok said quietly. "I learned things no child should know about survival, about what a human being can endure and still remain human. When we finally reached the markets of Goa, I was no longer the boy who had planted seeds beside his mother. I was something harder, like iron—something forged, but not from heat, but from suffering."

His rowing companion had grown quiet, sensing the weight of what he was hearing. The storm continued to rage above them, but in the space between their words, it seemed to fade into background noise.

"But here's what I learned," Majok continued, a note of something approaching hope entering his voice. "My mother's lessons about bringing dead things back to life—they weren't just about plants. They were about people too. No matter how broken you become, no matter how dead you feel inside, there's always the possibility of new growth. You just have to be patient, and you have to believe that somewhere, in some season you can't yet imagine, the rains will come again."

1577

"By the time I reached my twentieth year, I had been recruited into the military caste known as the Habshi," Majok continued, his stroke pattern shifting slightly as the memory carried him forward through time. "Habshi—an Arabic word for African people living in India. We were valued for our strength, our size, and our ability to intimidate enemies before the fighting even began."

The man beside him looked up with newfound respect. "You were a soldier?"

"I was a trained killer," Majok corrected, his voice matter-of-fact. "And I was very good at it. So much so that I found favor in the eyes of my Indian master, a man named Rajesh Gupta who controlled a network of trading posts along the western coast. My success in his service earned me certain privileges—hot meals when others ate scraps, wine when others drank brackish water, and women when others slept alone."

But even as he spoke of these rewards, Majok's expression softened, as if touching on something far more precious than material comfort. "It was during this time that I met her," he said, and for the first time since beginning his story, his rowing faltered slightly. "Amara. Her name meant 'eternal' in her language, and looking at her, I understood why her parents had chosen it. She had been brought to India from somewhere near the Horn of Africa—Ethiopia, perhaps, or Somalia. She had the high cheekbones and elegant features of her people, but it was her eyes that captured me. They held starlight."

Majok's companion sensed they were approaching the heart of the story, the wound that still bled despite the years that had passed.

"We were not allowed to marry," Majok continued. "Slaves could not enter into formal unions—that privilege was reserved for free men. But we could consummate our bond in the eyes of whatever gods were watching, and in our hearts, that was enough. We found a small room above a spice merchant's shop, a space barely large enough for a sleeping mat and a cooking pot, but it was ours."

The ship lurched particularly violently, and Majok's grip tightened on his oar, using the motion to drive his memories forward.

"Amara had knowledge of herbs and healing—skills that made her valuable to Gupta beyond her beauty. She treated the wounds of his soldiers, prepared medicines for his household, and slowly, carefully, began to build a reputation that afforded her a measure of protection. We lived quietly, carefully, always aware that our happiness existed at the sufferance of others." Majok sighed, then continued. "Before long, we were blessed with a daughter," Majok said, and his entire demeanor transformed. The hardness that had marked his recounting of slavery and warfare melted away, replaced by something tender and fierce. "We named her Nyota Angavu, which means 'bright star' in her mother's tongue. She was a beacon in the darkness of our world—a living reminder that even in the most unlikely places, beautiful things could grow." He paused in his rowing entirely for a moment, his eyes fixed on something far beyond the ship's wooden walls. "She had her mother's eyes and her father's stubborn chin. Even as an infant, she would fix you with a stare that seemed to see straight through to your soul. When she laughed—and she laughed often, despite the circumstances of her birth—it was like music that could make you forget, for just a moment that you were not free."

"Free to love," the man said abruptly, with bitterness in his tone that Majok could not deny, but only relate to."

"For three years, we lived as much like a family as circumstances would allow. I would return from campaigns to find Amara teaching our daughter the names of stars, or showing her how to grind spices, or singing her the old songs that connected her to a homeland she had never seen. In those moments, I could almost forget that we were property rather than people."

The storm was beginning to abate slightly, and through the lessening noise, both men could hear the sound of activity on the deck above—voices calling out instructions, the creak of rigging being adjusted.

"What happened?" his companion asked, though he seemed almost afraid to hear the answer.

Majok resumed his rowing, but his strokes had taken on a different quality—harder, more determined, as if he were pulling not just against the ocean but against the tide of memory itself. "What always happens," he said grimly. "Someone decided our happiness was an inconvenience."

The marketplace in Goa bustled with the controlled chaos that marked all successful trading centers. Merchants hawked their wares in a dozen languages while ships from across the Indian Ocean disgorged cargo that would soon make its way to markets from Lisbon to Manila. The air was thick with the scent of cardamom and black pepper, sandalwood and sea salt, and underneath it all, the particular smell of human commerce—sweat and desperation and the peculiar tension that arose whenever people were being bought and sold.

Majok stood on a raised platform beside his master, Rajesh Gupta, while two European men examined him with the calculating gazes of those accustomed to evaluating livestock. One was clearly Portuguese—his olive skin and dark hair marking him as a man of the colonies, probably born in Goa to parents who had themselves come from Lisbon. He wore the practical clothing of a trader, but the quality of the fabric and the gold at his throat spoke of considerable success.

The other man was different entirely. Italian, by his accent and bearing, but there was something about him that set him apart from the typical merchants and adventurers who found their way to India's shores. He wore the simple black robes of a Jesuit priest, and his eyes—intelligent, compassionate, but also calculating—suggested a man accustomed to wielding a different kind of power than mere wealth.

"His combat record is impressive," Gupta was saying, gesturing toward a scroll that detailed Majok's service. "Seventeen campaigns, no defeats. He speaks Portuguese and Arabic in addition to his native tongues, and he has proven capable of command in the field. More importantly, he is absolutely loyal."

The Portuguese trader, who had introduced himself as Pedro Carvalho, nodded approvingly. "He's certainly large enough to intimidate. And you say he has family?"

"A woman and child," Gupta confirmed. "Which ensures his cooperation. A man with nothing to lose is dangerous. A man with everything to lose is controllable."

Alessandro Valignano, the Jesuit, said nothing, but his eyes remained fixed on Majok's face, as if trying to read something written there in a language only he could understand.

"I have specific requirements," Carvalho continued. "My operations extend beyond simple trading. There are... entertainment venues... that cater to certain tastes among the Portuguese community. A man of his size and exotic appearance would be quite valuable in that capacity."

Something cold settled in Majok's stomach at these words, but he kept his expression neutral. He had learned long ago that showing emotion during such negotiations only complicated matters.

"Additionally," Carvalho went on, "the woman and child could be incorporated into the business as well. There are always customers interested in... variety."

The words hit Majok like physical blows, but still he remained motionless. Beside him, Gupta nodded as if the Portuguese trader had merely commented on the weather.

"That would, of course, require a higher price," Gupta said.

It was then that Valignano stepped forward, his movement drawing all eyes to him.

"Perhaps," he said quietly, "we might discuss an alternative arrangement."

Carvalho's eyes narrowed slightly. "Father, surely you're not interested in competing for this particular asset? The Church has little use for warriors of his... capabilities."

"On the contrary," Valignano replied smoothly. "I am about to undertake an extensive journey through territories where the safety of Christian missionaries cannot be guaranteed. A man of proven loyalty and martial skill would be invaluable as a bodyguard."

"I'm prepared to offer three thousand ducats," Carvalho said quickly. "Plus an additional thousand for the woman and child."

Valignano appeared to consider this, then shook his head. "Five thousand ducats. For the man alone."

The sum was staggering—enough to purchase a small ship or finance a trading expedition. Gupta's eyes widened, while Carvalho's face darkened with anger. "Father, you're being absurd. No bodyguard is worth such a sum."

"Perhaps not," Valignano agreed. "But a man's soul often is."

As the two Europeans argued over terms, Valignano caught Majok's eye and gestured almost imperceptibly toward a shaded area near the edge of the marketplace. Understanding the signal, Majok moved quietly away from the haggling voices. A few chickens rustled across the ground as Majok slammed in close and leaned down to hear what Valignano had to say.

"Walk with me," Valignano whispered, when Majok joined him. They moved through the crowd until they reached a small tea shop where the noise of the marketplace faded to a manageable level.

"You understand Portuguese," Valignano observed. It was not a question.

"Yes, Father."

"And your mastery of English is as good, I suppose?"

"It is the popular tongue, is it not?"

"Indeed. Hmm," Valignano considered him closely as silence hung between them. "Then you heard what that man intends for you and your family."

Majok's jaw tightened, but he nodded.

"Last night, I was staying at the inn where many of the Portuguese traders lodge," Valignano continued. "I overheard Senhor Carvalho speaking quite freely about his plans for you. His establishment caters to men whose appetites run toward... violence and degradation. He spoke of using your size to intimidate his customers into compliance, and of your family as additional entertainment for those whose tastes run toward the truly depraved."

The words confirmed Majok's worst fears, but hearing them spoken aloud by this compassionate priest somehow made them more bearable, as if sharing the burden made it lighter.

"If I am able to purchase you," Valignano said carefully, "it will void Carvalho's interest entirely. More importantly, I can arrange for your family to be placed under the protection of certain associates of mine here in India—men who owe favors to the Society of Jesus and who can ensure their safety."

"And in return?" Majok asked.

"You would serve as my bodyguard for a period of three years. I have trading routes and missionary work that will take us far from India—to Macau, to the Philippines, and eventually to Japan. But I give you my word that when my work is complete, you will be reunited with your family as a free man."

Majok studied the priest's face, looking for signs of deception and finding none. "Why would you do this?"

"Because," Valignano said simply, "every man deserves the chance to protect what he loves."

They returned to find that Gupta had accepted Valignano's offer, much to Carvalho's obvious fury. The Portuguese trader's face was flushed with anger as gold changed hands, and when the transaction was complete, he stormed away without a word.

"I've seen this type before," Valignano murmured to Majok as they watched Carvalho disappear into the crowd. "That one will not let this go unchecked. We must make plans to leave tomorrow, and quickly."

"Tomorrow?" Majok asked, thinking of Amara and Nyota Angavu.

"I have sea routes that will take us through the Strait of Malacca to Macau, then north along the China coast to Japan. We will be out of India for some time, but we will return for your family. With the money we make, I will barter for their freedom. As my bodyguard, if you work out as I anticipate you will, you'll be a free man with your family when our contract is complete. I give you my word."

Majok looked into the priest's eyes and saw something he had almost forgotten existed—genuine compassion coupled with unshakeable resolve. For the first time in years, he allowed himself to hope.

"I understand, Father. When do we sail?"

"At dawn," Valignano replied. "Make your farewells tonight, but be ready. I suspect Senhor Carvalho is not the sort of man who accepts defeat gracefully."

Chapter 5: The Japa

The attack came in the darkest hour before dawn, when even the most vigilant sentries struggled against the weight of sleep. Majok's eyes snapped open at the first sound—not the crash of splintering wood or the ring of steel, but something subtler and far more ominous: the soft whisper of sandaled feet moving with predatory stealth across the packed earth outside their lodging.

He had chosen to spend his final night in India not in the comfortable quarters Valignano had secured near the harbor, but in the cramped room above the spice merchant's shop where Amara and Nyota Angavu waited for him. The space was barely large enough for the three of them, but it held all the warmth and love his world contained.

Now, as shadows moved beyond the thin wooden walls, Majok felt that world beginning to collapse. "Amara," he whispered, his hand finding her shoulder in the darkness. "Wake up. We have visitors."

She came alert instantly—three years of living as property had taught them both to surface from sleep like warriors. Her hand moved to cover their daughter's mouth before Nyota Angavu could make a sound, and in the dim starlight filtering through their single window, Majok saw his own fear reflected in his wife's eyes.

The first torch appeared at the base of the building, its orange light dancing against the walls like a harbinger of destruction. Then came Carvalho's voice, thick with wine and rage.

"I know you're in there, African! You and that priest think you can humiliate Pedro Carvalho? Think you can steal what should be mine?" A pause, then laughter that held no humor whatsoever. "I have twenty men with me, and we're not leaving until we've settled accounts."

Through the cracks in the floorboards, Majok could see more torches gathering in the narrow alley below. The Portuguese trader had indeed come in force, and the men with him bore the look of seasoned killers—mercenaries and slavers who would think nothing of burning a building to reach their quarry.

"There's another way out," Amara whispered, gesturing toward a window that faced the back of the building. "The roof of the bakery next door—we could make it if we move quickly."

But even as she spoke, they heard voices from that direction as well. Carvalho had been thorough in his planning.

"No," Majok said quietly. "They have us surrounded." He moved to the window facing the street and peered down at the gathering crowd. "But they haven't seen Valignano yet."

As if summoned by his words, the priest appeared at the mouth of the alley, flanked by two men whose bearing marked them as soldiers despite their civilian clothes. Alessandro Valignano walked with the measured pace of a man accustomed to authority, showing no fear despite being outnumbered ten to one.

"Senhor Carvalho," Valignano called out, his voice carrying easily through the pre-dawn air. "This is most irregular. Surely you don't intend to conduct business at this hour?"

"Business?" Carvalho's laugh was harsh and bitter. "You cost me four thousand ducats tonight, priest. That's not business—that's theft."

"I offered a higher price for goods fairly offered for sale," Valignano replied calmly. "That's not theft. That's commerce."

"You had no right!" Carvalho's voice cracked with fury. "I had an agreement with Gupta! You swooped in like some carrion bird and—"

"I exercised my right as a free agent in an open market," Valignano interrupted. "If you have a complaint about the legality of the transaction, I suggest you take it up with the Portuguese authorities in the morning."

Above them, Majok was already moving. He pressed a small carved baby elephant into Nyota Angavu's palm—a toy he had made for her third birthday. He flashed another one at her, a larger one, and twice the size of hers. Both miniatures were carved from a single piece of ivory that had cost him a week's wages. Connected to each one was a single strange of leather tassel. Majok donned his necklace over his head as Nyota Angavu did the same.

"Listen to me, bright star," he whispered, kneeling so that his eyes were level with hers. "Papa has to go away for a while, but this will help you remember me. And when I come back, we'll unite our elephants again—he papa with the daughter. And then we will go somewhere safe, somewhere no one can ever separate us again."

Nyota Angavu's eyes, so much like her mother's, filled with tears she was too young to understand. "Papa, why can't you come with us?"

The question hit him like a large anvil, as his chest tightened with she spoke. But it was less her words, but the tone and the painful undertone in her voice. But before he could answer, the smell of smoke began to drift through their window.

"They're burning the building," Amara said, her voice tight with controlled panic.

Below, Carvalho's voice rose to a roar. "If I can't have what I paid for, then no one can! Burn it all!"

Majok moved to the window and saw flames already licking at the base of the structure. Carvalho's men had doused the lower level with oil, and the old wood was catching with terrifying speed.

"The roof," he said urgently. "Now."

They climbed through the back window onto the sloping tiles of the spice merchant's roof, Majok carrying Nyota Angavu while Amara clutched the small bundle of possessions that represented their entire life together. The heat from below was already intensifying, and smoke was beginning to pour through the gaps in the tiles.

But Carvalho had indeed planned thoroughly. As they reached the edge of the roof, men emerged from the shadows of the neighboring buildings. Majok counted at least six, all armed, all moving with the coordinated precision of professional killers.

"Well, well," called one of them, a scarred man with Portuguese features and the lean build of a ship's fighting man. "Look what we have here."

What happened next unfolded with the brutal efficiency that had made Majok valuable to his former master. He set Nyota Angavu gently on the roof tiles, kissed the top of her head, and stepped forward to meet the approaching men.

The first attacker came at him with a curved blade, the kind of fighting knife favored by sailors in close quarters. Majok caught the man's wrist, twisted until bone snapped, and drove his knee into the attacker's solar plexus with enough force to lift him off his feet. The knife clattered away into the darkness.

The second man tried to circle behind him, but Majok spun with fluid grace, his massive hand closing around the man's throat. He lifted the struggling figure clear off the ground and hurled him from the roof. The scream that followed was cut short by the wet sound of impact.

But it was the third attacker who made the fatal mistake. Instead of engaging Majok directly, he lunged toward Nyota Angavu, perhaps thinking to use the child as leverage.

Majok's roar of rage seemed to shake the very foundations of the building. He covered the distance between them in two strides, his hands closing around the man's head. What followed was swift and terrible—a sharp twist, the sickening crunch of vertebrae separating, and the attacker's body went limp as a rag doll.

The remaining three men hesitated, suddenly aware that they were facing not just a large man, but a predator whose family had been threatened.

It was then that Valignano appeared, climbing through a window from the building next door. Behind him came his two companions, and the sudden arrival of reinforcements tipped the balance decisively.

"This way!" Valignano called, gesturing toward a rope that had been secured to the roof's peak. "My ship is anchored just beyond the harbor mouth!"

As they made their way down the rope, Majok could see that the entire spice merchant's quarter was now ablaze. Carvalho's desire for vengeance was consuming far more than just their tiny room—dozens of families would be homeless by morning, countless livelihoods destroyed.

At the base of the building, Valignano's men had horses waiting. "You'll have to split up," the priest said urgently. "Take your family to the ship—my men will escort you. Once there, you will board, but your family will have to stay behind. I'll create a distraction to draw Carvalho's attention."

"Father—" Majok began.

"No arguments," Valignano said firmly. "The ocean is no place for a woman and child, especially with hostile ships in pursuit. My associates will take them to a safe house inland. When we return from Japan, we'll collect them." The words made sense, but they felt like a sentence of death nonetheless.

"Come, follow me!" Majok urged his family as they all scurried through the night in the direction of the harbor. When they arrived, Majok knelt before Nyota Angavu one final time, his hands trembling as he cupped her small face.

"Papa has to go on a big ship," he said, his voice barely steady. "But I promise—I swear to you by all the stars in the sky—that I will come back for you."

"When?" she asked, her lower lip trembling.

"Soon, bright star. Very soon."

But as Amara tried to pull their daughter away, Nyota Angavu broke free and wrapped her small arms around Majok's leg, clinging with the desperate strength of a child who sensed that something irreversible was happening.

"Papa, why can't you come on the boat with us?" she sobbed. "I don't want you to go away!"

Majok felt his heart breaking as he gently loosened her grip, lifting her into his arms one last time. He breathed in the scent of her hair, memorized the weight of her small body against his chest, tried to burn every detail into his memory.

"Because sometimes," he whispered, "papas have to do dangerous things to keep their bright stars safe. But no matter how far away I go, no matter how long I'm gone, I will always find my way back to you. That's what papas do."

Amara stepped forward, her own eyes bright with unshed tears. She placed her hand on Majok's cheek and spoke words in her native tongue—words of love and blessing and desperate hope.

Then she took Nyota Angavu from his arms, and Majok felt a piece of his soul tear away.

The last thing he saw as they disappeared into the darkness was his daughter's small hand waving goodbye, the carved elephant clutched in her fingers as it hung from her neck, like a talisman against the uncertainties that lay ahead.

The sea chase that followed would be remembered by sailors in Goa's taverns for years to come. Carvalho, his rage undimmed by the destruction he had already wrought, commandeered three fast vessels and gave pursuit the moment he realized his quarry had escaped.

Valignano's ship—a sleek caravel built for speed rather than cargo—cut through the pre-dawn swells with the grace of a seabird. But behind them, Carvalho's vessels gained steadily, their crews driven by the promise of gold and the fear of their captain's wrath.

Majok stood at the bow, his hands gripping the rail as he watched the Indian coastline shrink into memory. Somewhere behind them, lost in the darkness, Amara and Nyota Angavu were being carried to safety. He had to believe that. He had to trust that Valignano's associates were as reliable as the priest claimed.

But as the Portuguese ships drew closer, their intentions became clear. This was not a chase—it was a hunt, and Carvalho meant to end it with blood.

The first cannon shot thundered across the water just as the sun crested the horizon, the ball splashing into the waves mere yards from their stern. Valignano's captain, a weathered Genoese named Marco Santori, began shouting orders in three languages as his crew scrambled to coax more speed from their vessel.

"Can we outrun them?" Majok asked.

Santori spat over the side and shook his head. "In open ocean, maybe. But they know these waters better than we do. They'll try to herd us toward the reefs."

Another cannon shot, closer this time. Majok could see Carvalho himself standing in the bow of the lead vessel, his face twisted with rage even at this distance.

It was then that Valignano appeared beside them, his priest's robes replaced by the practical clothing of a sea-going man. "There's a storm building to the west," he said, pointing toward a line of dark clouds on the horizon. "If we can reach it before they overtake us..."

"That's a monsoon front," Santori protested. "We could be torn apart."

"We'll certainly be torn apart if we stay here," Valignano replied calmly.

For the next two hours, they raced toward the approaching storm while Carvalho's ships closed the distance. Cannon shots fell around them with increasing frequency, and twice the ship shuddered as Portuguese balls found their mark. But Santori's crew knew their business, and gradually, incrementally, they began to pull ahead.

But one ship in particular, the Norris closed in utilizing thrust engine technology—a controversial form of energy that fuels jets mounted on the stern of the vessel—to get dangerously within cannon range.

"Captain, Norris off the port bow," a voice from one of the crew cried aloud.

Santori raced to the side of the boat to get a good look at the ship. The body of a naked woman dressed in a flowing dressed kissed the bow of the enemy vessel. His eyes grew wide. Santori mumbled something in his native tongue that Valignano recognized a deity similar to his god of Christian belief. He knew they were in trouble now. "We need to fight back. How about our cannon?"

Santori turned to face him. "If it still works. We haven't fired it in years.

"But, what choice do we have?" Valignano asked.

Santori nodded over to one his crew who was looking on, wearing a face of equal desperation to that of his captain. "Quickly, get a few men and fasten the cannon to the starboard side of the ship where the Norris is. And quickly, we only have one shot at this!"

The men made haste and secured the cannon to the ship, aimed squarely at the Norris. As they loaded the cannonball in, Santori noted something concerning. "Only one?"

"Yes, captain," the crewman said.

"We will have to shoot straight," Valignano said.

Santori crouched behind the cannon, squinting down the iron sight as he tried to calculate distance and trajectory. The Norris was closing fast, its controversial thrust engines sending jets of steam and smoke trailing behind it like the breath of some mechanical dragon. He could see Carvalho's men preparing their own cannon, the Portuguese trader himself standing at the bow with a look of murderous satisfaction.

"Steady now," Santori muttered, his finger hovering over the firing mechanism. "One shot, one chance..."

The sound hit them first—a thunderous boom that seemed to shake the very air around them. Carvalho's cannon had fired, and Santori could hear the distinctive whirr of the cannonball cutting through the morning air, growing louder as it approached.

The splash came directly in front of their bow, sending a towering column of seawater cascading across the deck. The shock of it—the proximity, the realization of how close death had come—caused Santori's hand to jerk involuntarily.

His cannon fired with a deafening roar, the recoil sending him stumbling backward. Through the acrid smoke, he watched in dismay as their precious cannonball arced high over the Norris, missing the ship entirely and splashing harmlessly into the ocean beyond.

"Merda!" Santori cursed, slamming his fist against the cannon's barrel. "We're done for!"

But even as the words left his mouth, something impossible happened. The Norris, which had been bearing down on them with lethal intent, suddenly erupted in a ball of orange flame. The explosion seemed to come from nowhere—a violent bloom of fire that consumed the ship's midsection in seconds. The thrust engines died with a mechanical scream, and the vessel began to list heavily to starboard.

Majok, who had been watching from the bow, felt something stir deep in his chest—a warmth that had nothing to do with the distant flames. For just a moment, the air around him seemed to shimmer with heat distortion, and he could have sworn he heard something like distant drums beating in rhythm with his heart.

"How—?" Valignano stared at the burning ship in amazement. "Our shot missed completely!"

Santori crossed himself, his weathered face pale with shock. "Sometimes," he said quietly, "the gods favor the righteous."

As they watched, the Norris settled deeper into the water, its crew abandoning ship while Carvalho's other vessels moved to assist the survivors. The chase was over—not through superior seamanship or lucky shooting, but through what could only be called divine intervention.

Majok touched his chest where the warmth still lingered—hovering just below the ivory elephant—wondering at the strange sensation. Somewhere, in a realm beyond mortal understanding, ancient forces were stirring—and somehow, impossibly, they seemed to be on his side.

When they finally reached the storm front, the wind hit them like some magical, invisible force. The sea transformed from blue-green swells into towering walls of gray-green water, and rain began to fall in sheets that made it impossible to see more than a few yards in any direction.

Behind them, the remaining Carvalho's ships vanished into the chaos, their captains forced to choose between pursuit and survival.

For three days, they battled the storm, taking turns at the oars when the wind failed them, working together as men who knew their lives depended on each other's strength. And when the weather finally cleared, they found themselves alone on an empty ocean, as his service to Valignano unofficially began, along with adventure and uncertainty somewhere beyond the northern horizon.

"*There*, that should be enough," Majok said, straightening from his rowing position as the memory of that storm faded back into the present. "Take your break. There is wine in the aft."

His rowing companion stared up at him in amazement as Majok's true size became apparent. Standing, he towered over the other men in the ship's belly, his shoulders broad enough to block out the lamp that swung overhead.

"You're not—" the man began.

"A slave?" Majok smiled, but there was sadness in it. "No. Not anymore."

"I figured as much. You were way too calm," the man said.

"You're correct. And as you are now aware from the story, it's not the first storm I've been through," Majok replied with a proud grin.

He made his way through the ship to the bow, where Alessandro Valignano stood watching the horizon. The sun hung in the sky, peaking from behind the clouds, filling the sky with splashes of yellow, red, orange and blue light that competed for attention. Years on the open ocean had painted beautiful canvases a myriad of times, with each one burning a vista of beauty in Majok's mind that never seemed to grow old.

The priest turned as Majok approached, offering him a wooden cup filled with wine mixed with water. Standing beside the priest, Majok's height advantage was striking—eight or nine inches at least. "Your ceaseless motivation of the men is remarkable," Valignano observed, staring up at his faithful bodyguard.

"I learned from the best," Majok replied.

"No," Valignano shook his head. "The mantle of leadership cannot be learned. Cultivated, maybe, but not taught. You are a leader of men, and one day, you will lead hundreds, perhaps thousands."

"You humble me, sir. I have no desire to do such things."

"Desire has nothing to do with it. It's your calling, trust me."

Majok took a sip of the wine, feeling its warmth spread through his chest. "Well, I am only motivated by my will to rejoin my family."

"And one day you shall return," Valignano said firmly. "I gave you my word."

It was then that one of the ship's officers approached, his face bright with excitement. "Sir, land mass over the port bow, approximately fifteen nautical miles distant."

Valignano smiled, the expression transforming his weathered features. "Excellent. Prepare the ship for arrival." He looked over to Majok, and in his eyes was the gleam of a man about to embark on a grand adventure. "Japan awaits."

Chapter 6: The Settei

The morning sun painted the deck in shades of gold and amber as Majok stood beside Alessandro Valignano, watching the coastline of Japan emerge from the ocean mist like something from a dream. After two years of service, he had grown accustomed to the priest's contemplative silences, but today something felt different—there was an energy about Valignano that spoke of excitement barely contained.

"Today is your day, Majok," Valignano said finally, his eyes fixed on the approaching harbor. "I have some insight on a new trade route that will take us through Indonesia and on to the Philippines."

"The Philippines?" Majok asked, his interest piqued despite himself. "What trade commodities do they have to offer?"

"The noblest kind. Information, sir." Valignano's smile carried the gleam of a man who had discovered something valuable. "The Philippines are a wondrous place, with all kinds of peculiar and fascinating creatures native to those islands. Many people will pay considerable coin for documentation on these animals, along with detailed maps of the trade routes. But more than that, there are a great many converts ascending from the Philippines, people I'd very much like to make acquaintances with for the future of our mission work."

Majok nodded, though his mind was already racing ahead to more personal concerns. "And this information you seek—it's available in Japan?"

"Japan houses some of the largest groups of missionaries outside of Europe itself. My contacts here will have all the information we need." Valignano paused, then turned to face Majok directly. "But more importantly to you, this venture will take the majority of the next year—which is all that remains on your contract with me. And thus, once we finish this route, I will return you to India to reunite with your family."

The words hit Majok like a physical blow, though not an unpleasant one. Hope, so long held in careful check, suddenly blazed in his chest. "It's already been two years?"

"Yes, indeed," Valignano confirmed, and there was genuine warmth in his voice. "You've been an incredible bodyguard, but more importantly, a friend as well. You may not see it that way, and you don't owe it to me to say you feel the same, but I have enjoyed our escapades and your companionship, sir."

The priest reached out and clapped Majok's shoulder with the easy familiarity of shared hardships and mutual respect.

Majok felt the weight of honesty settling on him like a mantle. "I'm sorry, but it is difficult to share the same sentiments. You've been fair and good to me, but my focus remains on my family."

Almost unconsciously, his hand moved to clutch the ivory elephant that dangled around his neck, the carved papa elephant that connected him across impossible distances to the bright star of his heart.

"I'm sure you understand," he finished quietly.

"Yes, I do, more than you know," Valignano replied, and something flickered behind his eyes—a shadow of personal loss that hinted at stories he had never shared. "One day, we will share stories. But for now—"

"I don't have stories," Majok interrupted, his voice carrying a weariness that spoke of more than physical exhaustion. "All I have are my memories, which seem to grow hazier by the day. Some of which have blended with my dreams. I find it difficult nowadays to comprehend which is real or imagined."

Valignano studied his face for a long moment, then smiled with the gentle understanding that had made him such an effective missionary. He took Majok by both arms, giving him a gentle but firm squeeze. "Well, if you want some advice, I say hold on to all of it. Dreams are good. Dreaming is what keeps us alive. Your day will come soon enough, you'll see."

As if summoned by his words, the ship's captain began shouting orders as they approached the harbor proper. The port of Sakai spread before them like a living tapestry of commerce and culture, a sight that never failed to impress even seasoned travelers.

The harbor teemed with vessels of every description—sleek Chinese junks with their distinctive battened sails, Portuguese caravels similar to their own, local Japanese ships with their elegant lines and practical design. The docks groaned under the weight of trade goods from across the known world: sacks of precious spices from the Indies, bolts of silk that caught the morning light like captured rainbows, cages containing exotic animals whose cries added to the symphony of commercial activity.

Buddhist temple ships, distinguished by their ceremonial banners and the saffron robes of their passengers, occupied positions of honor near the harbor's center. The influence of Buddhism in Japan was unmistakable—from the architecture visible beyond the docks to the respectful way even hardened merchants made space for the religious vessels.

"Remarkable, isn't it?" Valignano observed as their ship maneuvered toward an open berth. "This single harbor represents the convergence of a dozen different cultures, all united in the pursuit of trade and, in some cases, spiritual enlightenment."

Majok nodded, taking in the organized chaos with the eyes of a man who had seen many ports but never one quite like this. The Japanese efficiency was evident in everything from the way cargo was loaded and unloaded to the systematic inspection of arriving vessels by officials in distinctive court dress.

Once they had made ground and disembarked, Valignano directed Captain Santori and his men to begin the process of resupplying their vessel while he and Majok prepared to venture into the town proper.

"Majok, come with me," Valignano said with a smile. "The office of the Jesuit priests is about half a mile into town. I'll be your guide."

As they walked through the bustling streets, Valignano took on the role of instructor, providing Majok with his first real education in Japanese society and culture.

"What you're seeing here," Valignano explained as they passed a group of merchants haggling over rice prices, "is the foundation of Japanese wealth. Rice isn't just food here—it's currency. A daimyo's power is measured not in gold or silver, but in koku of rice. One koku feeds one person for one year, so when they say a lord controls a domain worth 100,000 koku, they're describing both his wealth and the population he can support."

They paused to watch a procession of craftsmen carrying their wares to market—exquisitely forged katana, delicate ceramics that seemed to glow with inner light, textiles woven with patterns so intricate they resembled living art.

"The artisan guilds here are unlike anything in Europe," Valignano continued. "These men don't just practice their crafts—they elevate them to forms of spiritual discipline. A swordsmith doesn't merely forge steel; he communes with the essence of the metal itself. The results speak for themselves."

As they moved deeper into the town, the evidence of Japan's rapid development became even more apparent. Castle towns—jōkamachi—were springing up around the strongholds of various daimyo, creating urban centers that combined military necessity with commercial opportunity.

"The merchant class is growing," Valignano noted, gesturing toward a group of well-dressed traders conducting business near a tea house. "Despite the social stigma traditionally attached to commerce, trade networks are developing that span the entire archipelago. The old rigid hierarchies are beginning to show cracks, though most Japanese would never admit it openly."

Majok absorbed all of this information with the intensity of a man who understood that knowledge could mean the difference between success and failure, between life and death. But even as he learned about Japan's complex society, part of his mind remained focused on the ivory elephant resting against his chest and the promise of reunion that lay at the end of Valignano's final mission.

At almost the same moment, but from a very different perspective, another ship was making its approach to the same harbor. This vessel, however, commanded a level of attention and respect that dwarfed anything accorded to foreign traders or missionaries.

The moment the distinctive war banner became visible through the morning haze, dock workers began shouting warnings and clearing pathways. Merchants hastily moved their goods to safer positions, while officials who had been leisurely inspecting other vessels suddenly found urgent reasons to focus their attention elsewhere.

Oda Nobunaga had returned to Sakai.

The ship itself was a testament to both practical necessity and deliberate intimidation. Larger than most trading vessels, it carried not just cargo but a contingent of samurai whose very presence radiated barely controlled violence. At the bow stood two figures who commanded attention even among such impressive company.

Nobunaga himself had changed considerably from the young man who had once been dismissed as the Fool of Owari. At forty-seven, he possessed the lean, predatory build of a career warrior, but it was his eyes that truly marked him as dangerous. They held the cold calculation of a man who had learned to see enemies in shadows and opportunities in every conversation.

Beside him stood Akechi Mitsuhide, one of his most trusted generals, though the relationship between them carried undercurrents of tension that spoke to the complex dynamics of feudal loyalty.

"The campaign in Echizen exceeded expectations," Nobunaga was saying as their ship drew closer to the dock. "The Ikko-ikki resistance collapsed faster than our intelligence suggested it would. My men are performing above expectations—they understand now that mercy is a luxury we cannot afford in these times."

Akechi nodded, though his expression remained carefully neutral. "Your strategy of combining overwhelming force with strategic clemency has proven effective, Oda-sama. The surviving population will remember both your power and your potential for forgiveness."

"Exactly," Nobunaga replied, his voice carrying the satisfaction of a man whose theories had been proven correct. "Fear opens doors that diplomacy cannot touch, but the promise of fair treatment ensures they remain open. It's a balance that few of my contemporaries have mastered."

As the ship maneuvered toward its berth, Nobunaga's tone shifted to more immediate concerns. "Now, regarding our new venture into the slave trade—how are you finding the management of our current assets?"

The question struck Akechi like a slap, though he was careful not to let his reaction show on his face. "The five slaves are... manageable, my lord. Though I must confess, this is no job for a general. My training and experience are better suited to—"

"To what?" Nobunaga's voice carried a dangerous edge that made Akechi's next words crucial.

"If I am to become a daimyo one day—" Akechi began, then caught himself, but it was too late.

"If you are to what?" Nobunaga's question was deceptively quiet, but those who knew him recognized the warning in his tone.

Akechi felt the ground shifting beneath his feet. "Sorry, Oda-sama. I was just remarking that—"

"Careful that your ambition does not precede you in such matters," Nobunaga interrupted, his voice now carrying the full weight of his authority. "It could be interpreted as pride, and that always leads down a road of envy and betrayal. You wouldn't want your lord to suspect such things of you, would you?"

The reference was unmistakable. Nobunaga had not forgotten the lessons of his uncle's treachery, nor the bitter necessity of his brother's death. Every man in his service understood that loyalty was not assumed but continually tested.

"No, my lord. You are correct. You are the Minister of the Right, and you are a just daimyo. I apologize unreservedly."

"Good." Nobunaga's smile carried no warmth whatsoever. "Your place will be as general until I achieve the shogunate, and not a second before—and that only if I see you fit for the task. So in the meantime, show yourself in good faith and do only as I ask. Or, as my enemies have quickly learned, the wrath of the Dairokuten Maō is unmatched on earth and rivals that of hell itself."

The invocation of his demon lord persona sent a chill through everyone within earshot. Nobunaga had cultivated this reputation deliberately, understanding that fear of the supernatural could be as effective as fear of conventional military might.

Akechi remained silent and bowed deeply, but behind his subservient expression, something cold and calculating began to take shape. The humiliation of being relegated to slave management, combined with the harsh reminder of his subordinate position, planted seeds that would, in time, grow into something far more dangerous than mere resentment.

As their ship finally reached the dock and the gangplank was lowered, both men prepared to disembark into a Japan that stood on the brink of either complete unification or total chaos. Neither could have guessed that in that same harbor, at that very moment, walked a man whose presence would alter the course of both their destinies.

The stage was set for a meeting that would echo through the centuries, though the players themselves remained unaware that fate was drawing them inexorably toward each other through the crowded streets of Sakai.

Chapter 7: The Bicha

1579

The Jesuit office occupied a modest building near the center of Sakai, its Christian cross carved into the wooden lintel serving as both identification and declaration of faith in a land where foreign religions were viewed with cautious tolerance. Inside, the smell of incense and parchment created an atmosphere that reminded Majok of libraries and places of learning, though the conversations taking place were decidedly practical in nature.

Alessandro Valignano stood before a large map spread across a wooden table, speaking earnestly with a Japanese woman whose Christian name was Maria but whose bearing suggested she had been born to considerably higher station than her current humble circumstances might indicate.

"The route through the Banda Sea can be treacherous during the monsoon season," Valignano was saying, his finger tracing a path between scattered islands. "Are you certain the Portuguese traders you mentioned have successfully navigated those waters as recently as last month?"

"Yes, Father," Maria replied, her Portuguese heavily accented but clearly understandable. "Captain Fernandez brought his ship through the Moluccas just three weeks ago. He reported favorable winds and no significant storms, though he did warn that the situation can change quickly this time of year."

"And the route to Manila from there?"

"Well established. The Spanish have been using it regularly for their treasure fleets. You should have no difficulty, provided you carry the proper documentation."

Valignano nodded, making notes in the margin of the map with a quill that had seen considerable use. "The information about the indigenous peoples of the Philippines—the potential converts you mentioned—how reliable are your sources?"

"Very reliable, Father. The Augustinians have established several missions in the northern islands, and they report thousands of souls eager to hear the word of Christ. The documentation you seek about the local customs and languages is waiting for you in Manila."

While this conversation continued, Majok stood near a window, examining a collection of pamphlets that detailed various aspects of Christian doctrine. The text was in Portuguese, which he could read reasonably well after two years of service with Valignano, but his attention kept drifting to the activity visible through the window.

The street outside bustled with the organized chaos typical of Japanese commercial districts. Merchants arranged their wares with aesthetic precision, even the most humble vegetable vendor displaying his produce as if it were art. Children darted between the adult legs, playing games that seemed to involve considerable amounts of shouting and laughter.

It was one of these children who caught Majok's attention—a small boy who had apparently dropped something and was now searching frantically near the base of a persimmon tree that grew beside the Jesuit office. The child's distress was evident even from a distance, and Majok found himself drawn to investigate.

"Thank you for the information," Valignano was saying as Majok quietly stepped outside.

"Safe travels and Godspeed, brother," Maria replied.

"Godspeed, and may Christ be with you."

"And also with you," came the traditional response.

By the time Valignano finished his pleasantries and noticed Majok's absence, he found his bodyguard squatted down beside the persimmon tree, his massive frame somehow managing to appear non-threatening despite his size.

"Majok! What are you doing?" Valignano asked as he approached.

Majok stood, holding a perfectly round persimmon that had apparently fallen from the tree above. The fruit was at the peak of ripeness, its orange skin glowing like a small sun in the morning light.

"I think this is yours," Majok said gently, holding it out to the young boy who cowered nearby, clearly intimidated by the stranger's imposing presence.

The child stared up at Majok with wide eyes, torn between fear and the obvious desire to reclaim his lost treasure.

"Take it," Majok encouraged, his voice as soft as he could make it. "I'm not going to hurt you."

Tentatively, the boy reached out and accepted the persimmon, then immediately pointed at Majok with his free hand, his voice filled with amazement.

"Ookii, ookii!" he exclaimed, his young voice carrying clearly in the morning air.

Majok furrowed his brow, the unfamiliar syllables meaning nothing to him. He craned his neck toward Valignano with a questioning expression.

"What is he saying?"

Valignano's smile was just beginning to form when another voice answered from the periphery.

"Big," came the reply in Japanese, spoken with the authority of someone accustomed to being heard and obeyed.

Both Valignano and Majok turned toward the source of the voice, and Valignano's expression immediately transformed from mild curiosity to barely concealed alarm. His mouth dropped open in recognition, and he raised a frightful hand toward Majok while simultaneously dropping his head in a bow of respect.

Majok, read the priest's body language and quickly followed suit, though he had no idea why he was bowing or to whom. "What did he say?" Majok whispered, maintaining his bowed position.

"Big," Valignano replied softly, his voice tight with tension.

"Who is that?" Majok asked in a hushed tone.

Valignano slowly raised his head, his movements careful and deliberate. Standing before them was a man of medium height but commanding presence, his elaborate armor and the quality of his weapons marking him as someone of considerable importance. More telling were the six samurai who flanked him, their hands resting casually on their sword hilts in the universal gesture of men prepared for violence at a moment's notice.

"General Akechi," Valignano said, switching to Japanese and offering a deeper bow. "**Konnichiwa**."

Akechi Mitsuhide nodded acknowledgment of the greeting, his calculating eyes taking in every detail of both men before him. "**Konnichiwa**," he replied, then immediately launched into a conversation that excluded Majok entirely.

What followed was a lengthy exchange in rapid Japanese, and though Majok could not understand the words, he could read the emotional currents flowing between the two speakers. Valignano seemed increasingly uncomfortable as the conversation progressed, his responses becoming shorter and more strained. More troubling still was the way General Akechi kept glancing in Majok's direction, his gaze appraising and speculative.

The conversation seemed to reach a crucial point when Akechi's voice suddenly carried with unmistakable authority. Several armed guards from what was obviously a much larger force entered the area, moving with the coordinated precision of professional soldiers. Within moments, they had formed a loose circle around Majok, their positioning casual but unmistakably effective.

Majok's patience finally wore thin. He had been excluded from a conversation about what was clearly his own fate, surrounded by armed men whose intentions were unclear, and kept in ignorance by linguistic barriers that grew more frustrating by the moment. "Priest, what gives?" he called out to Valignano, his voice carrying an edge of demand that made several of the samurai tense.

Valignano turned toward him, and Majok was shocked to see that the priest's face had gone pale, his blue eyes wide with what appeared to be genuine fear. "He says that the daimyo is requesting your presence to serve," Valignano replied, his voice carefully controlled but unable to hide his distress.

"What does that mean?"

Valignano swallowed hard, the sound audible in the sudden quiet that had fallen over the street. "It means that you are to leave at once and accompany them to the compound in Owari."

The words hit Majok like a physical blow. After two years of faithful service, with only one year remaining on his contract, with reunion with Amara and Nyota Angavu so close he could almost taste it, he was being told that none of that mattered.

What followed was a rapid exchange between Valignano and Akechi, with the priest's voice taking on the tone of someone making a desperate plea. "**I must respectfully object to this man's departure**," Valignano said in Japanese, his Portuguese accent making the formal language sound stilted but determined. "**Kono otoko no shuppatsu ni taisuru gimon**."

Akechi's response carried the dangerous smoothness of a blade being drawn from its sheath: "**Sore wa dou iu imi desu ka?**"

"**Kare wa jiyu na otoko desu. Doreiwadewa arimasen**," Valignano insisted, then switched to Portuguese, perhaps hoping to make his point more clearly. "**This man cannot be purchased. He is a free man, not property to be bought and sold**."

Akechi's smile was cold and calculating. "**Good**," he replied in Portuguese that was surprisingly fluent. "**Then he will agree to come freely**." The general turned toward his men and spoke a single word that needed no translation: "**Tsurete ike!**"

Two of the samurai immediately moved to take Majok by the arms. Despite being surrounded, Majok still towered over every man present, his shoulders and biceps tensing instinctively as hands closed on him.

Valignano caught the movement and quickly stepped forward, his voice sharp with alarm. "No, sir! Please do not resist. You must not resist!"

"What is going on?" Majok demanded, his confusion and growing anger making his voice carry farther than he intended.

Before Valignano could fully explain, Akechi barked out an order that silenced all other conversation: "**Katoro tsu te iku!**"

The command was followed by immediate action as more soldiers moved to surround the group, their intent now unmistakably clear.

Valignano made one last desperate attempt to intervene, stepping directly into Akechi's path and blocking the route back toward the harbor. "**This man has not completed his financial obligation to me**," he said, his voice carrying all the authority he could muster. "**He still has one year remaining on his contract with the Society of Jesus**."

Akechi's eyes narrowed dangerously, and when he spoke, his voice carried the particular menace that came from a man who was accustomed to having his will obeyed without question. "**Tread softly, priest. You have strayed onto dangerous ground in two very distinct and precarious ways**." His hand moved to rest on his sword hilt, the gesture casual but unmistakable. "**First, you are a white man, and we do not trust white men in our lands. They have proven to be very... deceitful. Second, first you say he is a free man, and now you say quite the opposite. Your words bend and sway back and forth like a Japanese cherry tree. And when a tree sways too far, it rots away and bears no fruit. It is only good enough to be hewn down and used for fire**."

The threat was delivered with such calm precision that it seemed to freeze the very air around them. Valignano hands fisted at his side. At that moment he knew that he was ridiculously in over his head and resisted the urge to flinch.

Akechi drew his sword just far enough from its scabbard that the steel caught the morning light. "**The next words that come from your mouth will dictate what your fate will be**," he said quietly.

Valignano remained silent, his head dropping in defeat. The political reality was inescapable—he was a foreign priest in a foreign land, with no legal standing and no protection beyond what courtesy might provide. Against a general of Oda Nobunaga's army, courtesy was a fragile shield indeed. He turned slightly toward

Majok, and his whispered words carried all the weight of failed promises and shattered hopes. "I'm sorry."

The procession back to the harbor moved through streets that had somehow become empty of casual observers. Word traveled quickly in Sakai when Oda Nobunaga's forces were conducting business, and the local population had developed a survival instinct that kept them well clear of such operations.

Majok walked surrounded by samurai, his mind racing as he tried to process what had just occurred. Two years of faithful service, reduced to nothing by a conversation he couldn't understand and a decision he'd had no part in making. The ivory elephant around his neck seemed to grow heavier with each step, its carved surface a reminder of promises that now appeared impossible to keep.

As they ascended the gangplank to board Nobunaga's vessel, Majok's eyes swept across the main deck and locked onto a figure standing near the bow. Even at this distance, even without understanding the man's identity, Majok could feel the weight of that gaze burning into him with the intensity of flame.

Oda Nobunaga stood motionless, his eyes fixed on this new acquisition with the calculating attention of a predator evaluating potential prey. There was something in that stare—a mixture of curiosity and assessment—that made Majok wonder if this was someone he had somehow offended during his travels with Valignano, though he could not recall any such encounter.

Akechi barked something to his men, and they swiftly made a hard turn, taking Majok below deck rather than toward the figure on the bow. The stairs beneath Majok's feet creaked and moaned as if struggling to bear the weight of the large man, each step taking him deeper into the belly of the ship and further from the freedom he had been so close to grasping.

Finally, his journey came to a halt before a set of large wooden doors. A guard standing beside them produced a key and unlocked one of the heavy barriers, revealing nothing but darkness beyond.

They forced Majok inside, and the door slammed shut behind him with a finality that seemed to echo in his bones. He was immediately enveloped by complete darkness, pierced only by the cold and the sounds of heavy breathing and whimpering that told him he was not alone.

The familiar smells hit him then—unwashed bodies, fear, and desperation. It was a particular combination that marked places where human beings were kept as property rather than treated as people.

He recognized his circumstances completely. Despite Valignano's promises, despite two years of what he had thought was growing toward freedom, despite the contract that should have protected him, he was once again enslaved.

The ivory elephant around his neck seemed to pulse with its own weight, a tangible reminder of the family he had been so close to reuniting with, now separated from him once again by forces entirely beyond his control.

"Akechi!"

The voice that thundered across the ship's deck carried a authority that made even seasoned samurai straighten reflexively. Nobunaga's summons brooked no delay, and within moments, Akechi found himself bowing before his lord in the daimyo's private quarters.

The cabin was spartanly furnished but undeniably impressive, dominated by a low table where maps and documents were spread in organized precision. Nobunaga knelt behind the table, his posture relaxed but his eyes sharp with barely contained intensity.

"What exactly do you think you are doing?" Nobunaga demanded, his voice low but carrying the particular menace that his subordinates had learned to fear. "I commanded you to manage the slaves we already possess, not to acquire new ones through questionable means."

Akechi had prepared for this moment during the walk from the harbor, and his response was carefully crafted to appeal to his lord's particular combination of pragmatism and ambition. "My lord, what occurred today was not acquisition—it was recognition of opportunity," he began, his tone respectful but confident. "This man, Majok, has already become something of a legend among the people of Sakai. When he appeared in the street, crowds gathered just to observe him. Children pointed and stared. Even hardened merchants stopped their work to watch him pass." Nobunaga's expression remained impassive, but Akechi pressed on, sensing that he had his lord's attention. "Such a reaction can only be seen as a good omen for our cause. To have such a figure appear at the very moment when we are expanding our influence—surely the kami themselves are showing their favor toward your ultimate destiny."

"Continue," Nobunaga said, his voice giving away nothing of his thoughts.

"Among our other slaves, he will be a demonstration of your power and reach. When leaders from surrounding clans come to visit, they will see this man and wonder what other exotic resources you command. Their fear of you will grow because they will assume you have access to warriors and resources they cannot even imagine. Who knows what they will believe you might do with such advantages?"

Akechi paused for a moment, awaiting some form of acceptance of his story from Nobunaga, but the lord held his peace, barley batting an eye. After the brief moment passed, Akechi delivered what he hoped would be his most persuasive argument.

"It is psychological warfare, my lord," he said unwaveringly. "Without fighting a single battle, you will have planted seeds of doubt and fear in the minds of those who might otherwise oppose you. The Buddhist clans will surely second guess their continued resistance to your governing will."

Nobunaga was quiet for a long moment, his fingers drumming silently on the table as he considered his general's words. When he finally spoke, his voice carried the hard edge of a man who had not achieved his position through sentimentality. "You better be right in your assumptions. This cannot impede my primary objectives whatsoever," he said firmly. "My focus remains on solidifying my position and achieving the shogunate, along with further unifying Japan. Everything else—including exotic slaves and their supposed psychological impact—is secondary to that goal."

"Of course, my lord."

Nobunaga rose from his position and began to pace, his movements controlled but suggesting barely contained energy. "The clans will fear me because I am the Dairokuten Maō, the Demon King of the Sixth Heaven, not because I possess a tall slave." His voice grew harder with each word. "Need I remind you of the successes I have brought to Owari Province since becoming daimyo?" Without waiting for an answer, he began to enumerate his achievements, his tone taking on the cadence of a man reciting a litany of conquest. "I defeated the Saito clan and captured Mino Province, adding their resources to our own. I entered Kyoto and installed Ashikaga Yoshiaki as shogun, demonstrating our power to influence the highest levels of government. When that same Yoshiaki schemed against me, I expelled him, showing that my favor could be withdrawn as easily as it was granted."

He paused in his pacing, his eyes fixing on Akechi with laser intensity.

"I recall."

"I have begun the destruction of the powerful Takeda clan, and I will finish what I started there as well. These achievements speak to real power, Akechi. Not the illusion of power, but the substance of it."

Akechi bowed deeper, recognizing that his lord's patience was wearing thin. "You are absolutely correct, my lord. Your achievements speak for themselves, and no mere slave could add to such a legacy."

"Furthermore," Nobunaga continued, "you seem to have misunderstood your duties. You have not been relieved of your responsibilities regarding our existing slaves. You will continue to oversee both the old acquisitions and this new one. And if one thing goes awry under your watch—if there is so much as a whisper of trouble—your head will roll."

The threat was delivered with the casual certainty of a man who had followed through on such promises many times before.

"I understand completely, my lord," Akechi replied, though behind his subservient expression, something cold and calculating was taking shape. The humiliation of being reduced to a slave master, combined with the casual dismissal of his strategic insights, was adding fuel to resentments that had been building for over the last six years of his current nine year stint of servitude.

"Dismissed," Nobunaga said curtly, already turning his attention back to the maps spread across his table.

As Akechi left the cabin, his mind was already working through the implications of what had just occurred. His gambit had partially succeeded—Majok would remain in their possession—but the cost had been another layer of humiliation heaped upon his already considerable grievances against his lord.

Seeds of betrayal, like the ones he had mentioned to Nobunaga, could indeed take root in unexpected places.

In the darkness of the ship's hold, Majok sat with his back against the cold wooden wall, his hand instinctively clutching the ivory elephant that hung around his neck. The familiar weight of the carving was both comfort and torment—a reminder of love that now seemed impossibly distant.

Other figures moved in the shadows around him, and gradually his eyes adjusted enough to make out the shapes of perhaps a dozen other men, all bearing the particular posture of defeat that marked those who had been reduced to property. "You are new," a voice said quietly from nearby, speaking in accented Portuguese. "I am Kenji. What is your name?"

Majok turned toward the voice, making out the shape of a middle-aged Japanese man whose clothes suggested he had once held a position of some respect. "Majok," he replied, his voice barely above a whisper.

"You are now in the service of Oda Nobunaga," Kenji continued, his tone carrying the weary authority of someone who had learned hard lessons through bitter experience. "Daimyo of Owari Province, Dairokuten Maō—the Demon King of the Sixth Heaven—Udaijin, Minister of the Right, eighteenth head of the Oda clan." The litany of titles was delivered with the careful precision of a man who had memorized them as a matter of survival. "If you refuse to serve, you will be executed," Kenji added matter-of-factly. "That is not a threat. It is simply how things are."

Majok did not respond. He simply continued to back away until his shoulders met the wall, and then slowly sank down to the floor, his massive frame somehow managing to fold itself into the smallest possible space.

His fingers found the ivory elephant again, tracing the familiar curves of the carving that connected him to a daughter who was growing up without her father, to a woman who was waiting for a reunion that now seemed impossible to achieve.

In the darkness of the ship's hold, surrounded by the breathing of broken men and the creaking of timber, Majok held onto the one thing that remained of his humanity—the promise carved in ivory that one day, somehow, he would find his way back to those who loved him.

Even if that promise now seemed as fragile as the elephant itself.

Chapter 8: The Junbi

The journey from Sakai to the shores of Owari Province took the better part of a day, with Nobunaga's fleet cutting through waters that grew increasingly familiar as they approached the domain that had been shaped by three generations of Oda ambition. Majok, now chained alongside the other slaves in the ship's hold, could only glimpse fragments of the approaching coastline through the small portholes that provided the vessel's only natural light.

When they finally reached the small bay that served as the private harbor for the Oda compound, Majok felt the ship's movement change as they prepared to make anchor. The sound of chains and rope, the shouting of orders in Japanese, and the gradual settling of the vessel all spoke to a well-rehearsed operation—this was clearly not Nobunaga's first return to his stronghold.

As the gangplank was lowered and they were ordered to disembark, Majok got his first clear view of Owari Province. The bay was sheltered by rocky outcroppings that had been enhanced with man-made fortifications, creating a natural harbor that could be easily defended. Beyond the immediate coastline, rolling hills covered in dense forest stretched toward what appeared to be cultivated farmland, while in the distance, the distinctive silhouette of a castle complex dominated the horizon.

"Azuchi-jo," one of the Japanese slaves whispered to his companion, his voice carrying a mixture of awe and resignation. "Nobunaga's great castle."

Even from this distance, Majok could see that the structure was unlike anything he had encountered in his travels. Where European castles emphasized thick walls and defensive positioning, this Japanese fortress seemed to rise from the landscape like a natural formation, its multiple levels creating a graceful pyramid that spoke to both aesthetic sensibility and military practicality.

The procession from the harbor to the main compound followed a carefully maintained road that wound through terrain which had been shaped by generations of careful cultivation. Rice fields stretched in geometric precision across the flatter areas, while the hillsides were terraced to maximize agricultural yield. Everything Majok observed spoke to a level of organization and long-term planning that impressed him despite his circumstances.

Nobunaga himself rode at the head of the column, mounted on a stallion whose bloodlines were obviously as carefully maintained as everything else in this domain. He never once looked back at the slaves who followed in chains, his attention focused entirely on the path ahead and whatever business awaited him at his destination.

Akechi rode near the front as well, but Majok noticed that the general occasionally glanced back, his calculating gaze taking in every detail of their human cargo. There was something in those glances that suggested Akechi was already planning whatever came next.

As they approached the compound proper, Majok's architectural experience in India had not prepared him for what he now observed. The main complex was a masterwork of wooden construction that seemed to flow organically from the landscape around it. Multiple buildings were connected by covered walkways and arranged around courtyards that had been designed with the same attention to aesthetic harmony that marked every other aspect of Japanese culture he had observed.

The primary residence was clearly the largest structure, its curved rooflines and elaborate decorative elements marking it as the domain of someone with both wealth and refined taste. But what struck Majok most forcefully was how the entire complex seemed designed to exist in harmony with its natural surroundings rather than dominating them. Gardens flowed seamlessly between buildings, water features provided both beauty and practical function, and even the defensive positions were integrated so skillfully that they enhanced rather than detracted from the overall aesthetic.

As the main party approached the primary residence, Akechi gestured toward his men and spoke an order that resulted in the slaves being separated from the main group. Majok found himself being led away from the elegant main compound toward a cluster of smaller buildings that clearly served more utilitarian purposes.

The contrast was immediate and unmistakable. Where the main residence demonstrated wealth and aesthetic refinement, the slave quarters were purely functional. But even here, Majok noticed, the construction was solid and the maintenance was careful. These were not the squalid hovels he had grown accustomed to in other places—they were simply buildings designed for practical use rather than display.

To his surprise, Majok was not led to the largest of the slave buildings, where he could see the other captives being taken. Instead, his guards directed him toward a smaller, separate structure that stood somewhat apart from the others.

As they approached, Majok could see that this building was constructed in a style that reminded him of the training halls he had observed in India—a dojo, with walls that were more framework than solid barrier, allowing air and light to flow freely through the interior. The materials were traditional Japanese—wood and bamboo and rice paper—but the design emphasized openness and functionality over privacy or comfort.

The guards quickly removed his shackles and when they opened the door and gestured for him to enter, Majok stepped into a space that was surprisingly spacious and well-appointed. The floor was covered with tatami mats that showed signs of careful maintenance, and in the center of the room sat a large wooden tub that appeared to be carved from a single piece of timber and decorated with what looked like gold inlay.

Akechi appeared in the doorway and spoke to someone who remained outside, his voice carrying the tone of a man giving specific instructions.

"**The large one requires special preparation**," Akechi was saying in Japanese, unaware that his words would be understood by anyone listening. "**He is to be cleaned and groomed to meet the family standards. The lord wishes to evaluate this acquisition personally, and it would not do to present him in his current condition.**"

"**What specific preparations does the lord require**?" came a voice from outside—female, and carrying the tone of someone accustomed to managing such details.

"**Full cleansing, grooming to our standards, appropriate clothing**," Akechi replied. "**He will be presented to the family compound this evening, and he must be suitable for such an honor**."

As Akechi departed, Majok was left alone in the room, though he could hear quiet movement outside that suggested he was being watched. He was examining the craftsmanship of the wooden tub when he heard the soft tap-tap-tap of a walking stick approaching the entrance.

The man who entered was clearly advanced in years, moving with the careful but confident gait of someone who had long ago adapted to a significant disability. His walking stick was a thing of beauty—carved from what appeared to be hinoki cypress and polished to a warm golden sheen. But it was his face that immediately commanded attention. Scars crossed both eyes in parallel lines, speaking to some violent encounter that had taken his sight but clearly not his dignity.

Despite his blindness, the old man moved through the space with the assurance of someone who understood his environment completely. When he spoke, his voice carried the unmistakable cadence of education and authority.

"So, I take it you understand the popular tongue?" he asked in accented but fluent English.

Majok was so surprised to hear it, that for a moment he could not respond. Finally, he managed, "You speak English?"

The old man smiled, and despite the scars that marked his face, the expression was genuinely warm. "When you are as old as I am, you learn that adaptation is the key to survival. I am Ostrimyo, Wing to Lord Nobunaga. And you, I believe, are called Majok."

"You know my name?"

"I make it my business to know everything that might affect my lord's interests," Ostrimyo replied, settling himself gracefully onto one of the tatami mats. "And you, my large friend, have definitely affected his interests."

Majok felt a familiar surge of frustration and anger rising in his chest. "I never asked to affect anyone's interests. I was free, serving under contract, with only one year remaining before I could return to my family. Now I find myself in *these* chains again," he said as he paused to hold them up, as if the old man would be able to see them better, then he continued, "treated like property, with no say in my own fate."

"And this angers you," Ostrimyo observed. It was not a question.

"Of course it angers me! I am a man, not a tool to be passed from hand to hand according to the whims of those with power."

Ostrimyo nodded thoughtfully. "Your anger is understandable. Natural, even. But tell me—what good will that anger do you?"

"It preserves my pride, my sense of self as a human being rather than an object."

"Ah, pride," Ostrimyo said, his voice taking on the tone of a teacher preparing to make an important point. "And what of your family? You mentioned them. Tell me about this family you hope to return to."

Despite himself, Majok found his anger cooling slightly as thoughts of Amara and Nyota Angavu filled his mind. Almost without conscious decision, his hand moved to touch the ivory elephant that hung around his neck. "I have a woman," he said quietly. "Amara. And a daughter. Nyota Angavu—it means bright star. She would be..." he paused to calculate, "...nearly six years old now. If they are even still alive."

"You doubt their survival?"

"Two years is a long time to be protected only by the promises of others. And the world is not kind to those without power to defend themselves."

Ostrimyo was quiet for a moment, his scarred face turned toward Majok with an intensity that seemed to peer right through him despite his blindness. "So," he said finally, "you could choose the path of resistance. You could revolt, put up opposition to your new circumstances. But in the end, what would it gain you?"

"My dignity as a man rather than as property."

"True enough. But which is more important—your family or your *pride*?"

The question hung in the air like a blade waiting to fall. Majok knew the answer, but saying it aloud felt like a kind of surrender. "The answer is obvious," he said reluctantly. "But the chances of ever seeing them again seem to be growing slimmer by the day."

"Perhaps. But if you choose the path of resistance, it will end in your death. Trust me on this—I have seen what happens to those who openly defy Lord Nobunaga. And if you die here, what will that profit you? You will never see your family again, and they will never know what became of you."

"That seems to be inevitable anyway," Majok said bitterly.

"Only the will of the divine is truly inevitable," Ostrimyo replied. "Everything else offers choices, even when those choices are not immediately apparent."

Majok studied the old man's face, noting the way his scars caught the light filtering through the room's translucent walls. "And what about you? I see the scars. What *wise* choice did you make to deserve such a fate?" he asked mockingly. "Did your *divine power* help you when you needed it?"

To his surprise, Ostrimyo smiled. "I made the right choice and lived with the consequences."

"Doesn't look so right to me, old man. You don't have to agree just to win the argument. That would be *your* pride speaking."

Ostrimyo's smile widened, and he raised his hand to trace the scars across his eyes with his fingertips. "Only the ignorant need eyes to see clearly. I chose wisdom over sight, and it has been the better bargain. I may be blind, but I have never seen more clearly than I do now."

He extended his hands toward Majok. "Give me your hands."

Skeptical but curious, Majok extended his large hands toward the old man. Ostrimyo took them gently, his weathered fingers tracing the lines of Majok's palms with surprising delicacy. Suddenly, he gasped, his fingers stopping at certain points on Majok's skin. "Aww, as I thought. The marks on your hands," Ostrimyo said, his voice filled with something approaching joy. "These are signs of the Nhial-Majok—the sacred markings of abundance and protection."

Majok stared at the old man in shock. "How could you possibly know that? Those markings are from my people, the Dinka. I haven't heard those words spoken in over a decade."

"I am a scholar, Majok-san. I seek knowledge wherever it may be found, particularly knowledge of the hidden things that connect all peoples." Ostrimyo's voice took on the cadence of someone sharing profound wisdom. "Great is the man who fights for his life and dies with honor. But even greater is he who forgoes the battle that ends in certain death to await the struggle that offers the possibility of victory."

He paused, still holding Majok's hands. "As the caterpillar must die to its old self—the slow-moving, earthbound prey of every predator—to become the butterfly that can soar to new heights and experience realms of existence it could never have imagined, so must your path transform, my friend. That is, if you choose patience over recklessness."

Majok pulled his hands away and moved to the window, gazing out at the compound that had become his new prison. Through the translucent walls, he could see two women waiting patiently by the door, carrying baskets and containers that suggested they had been assigned to assist with whatever preparations Akechi had ordered.

"When my vision was taken from me," Ostrimyo continued, his voice soft but carrying clearly in the quiet room, "I, like you, fought against the frustration of what I had lost until it nearly destroyed me. Like you, my soul was drained and exhausted. There were mornings when it seemed miraculous that I could find the strength to rise from my bed."

"Then what changed?" Majok asked without turning from the window.

"I learned to listen," Ostrimyo said simply. "If I had not stopped fighting against my blindness, I would never have heard the sound of the hummingbird's wings as it visited me through the window of my room each morning. I would never have learned to hear the subtleties in the wind that tell of weather changes days in advance. It wasn't until I was able to calm my mind and embrace the stillness that I could perceive the calling of a new path." He paused, and when he spoke again, his voice carried the weight of hard-won wisdom. "Knowledge, embraced in place of fear and anger, gave me something far more powerful than what I had lost."

Majok turned from the window, studying the old man's scarred but peaceful face. "What was that?"

"Hope," Ostrimyo replied, then gestured toward the women waiting outside. "Let them do what they have been ordered to do. Allow yourself, for this moment, to embrace the possibility of a new path. It could be exactly what you need to restore that weary soul of yours for the journey ahead."

Majok looked toward the door, where the women waited with the patience of those accustomed to serving the needs of others. Finally, he sighed and began to remove his travel-stained clothing.

One of the women immediately moved to prepare the bath, adding heated water to the large tub until steam began to rise from its surface. The other gathered his discarded garments, handling even his worn and dirty clothes with a respect that surprised him.

As the woman working with the bath opened a wicker basket, Majok could see an array of items that spoke to a level of care he had not expected: soft towels woven from materials he could not identify, sponges that looked natural but felt impossibly soft, fresh mint leaves, honey that caught the light like amber, herbs whose scents reminded him of mountain meadows, and handmade soaps that appeared to contain milk, seaweed, clay, charcoal, hinoki oil, and what looked like persimmon.

When the bath was properly prepared, the women began adding the mint, honey, and herbs to the water. Almost immediately, the room filled with fragrances that seemed designed to calm the mind and ease the spirit. Despite his circumstances, despite his anger and frustration, Majok found himself breathing more deeply, his tense muscles beginning to relax.

As the scents reached his nostrils, something unexpected happened. The familiar combination of mint and honey triggered a memory so vivid it seemed to transport him across time and space. Suddenly, he could see his mother's face as clearly as if she stood before him—her gentle eyes, her patient smile, her hands as she had taught him to identify the plants that could heal and the ones that could harm.

Was this some form of Japanese magic? Somc calculated manipulation designed to weaken his resolve? But even as these suspicious thoughts crossed his mind, he remembered Ostrimyo's advice about embracing the moment rather than fighting it. This memory of his mother was a gift, regardless of how it had been triggered, and he would not squander it on paranoia.

With watery eyes, slowly, carefully, Majok's massive frame clearly requiring some accommodation. As the women stared at his newly naked physique in awe, he lowered himself into the bath. The warm water felt like a benediction against skin that had grown accustomed to discomfort and neglect. As the women began their work, their hands moving with professional skill across his shoulders and back, he felt layers of tension and grime being washed away.

The process was thorough beyond anything he had experienced. Working with gentle but persistent pressure, they scrubbed every inch of his skin until he was certain they had removed at least the top layer entirely. When they were satisfied with the condition of his body, they gestured for him to recline his head against the edge of the tub.

A basin was positioned to catch the water as one woman began pouring warm water from a pitcher across his forehead and scalp. The other worked her fingers through his hair, slowly and patiently loosening the coarse curls and locked strands that had grown increasingly tangled during his time at sea.

What followed was clearly the most complex part of the process. Both women coordinated their efforts with the precision of a practiced team, using various shampoos and oils to remove years of accumulated dirt and neglect. They rinsed and washed, refilled the pitcher and emptied the basin, repeating the process until they were satisfied that his hair was ready for the final stage.

The warmth of the water, the gentle pressure of their hands, and the lingering effects of the aromatic herbs combined to create a sense of peace that Majok had not experienced in years. Despite his intention to remain alert, he found himself drifting into sleep.

When he awoke, the women were putting the finishing touches on their work. Using creams and oils with techniques that seemed to blend practical necessity with artistic vision, they had created individual twists in his hair that somehow managed to echo the traditional nihongami styles favored by Japanese nobility while honoring the natural texture and character of his African heritage.

The result was unlike anything Majok had ever seen. His hair, rather than being forced into an alien shape, had been encouraged to take on a form that was both distinctively his own and somehow harmonious with Japanese aesthetic principles. The coarseness that had once seemed unmanageable now provided structure and stability, allowing the carefully crafted sections to hold their shape without the pins or combs that Japanese styles typically required.

When the women had completed their work, they bowed respectfully and withdrew, leaving a large, soft towel on a stool beside the tub. Majok rose from the bath, water streaming from his refreshed body, and reached for the towel.

As he dried himself, he noticed a polished metal mirror positioned in one corner of the room. Approaching it with curiosity, he studied his reflection for the first time in months. The man looking back at him was both familiar and transformed. His body, always powerful, now seemed to radiate health and vitality. His skin, freed from the accumulated grime of travel and captivity, had regained the rich darkness that had marked him among his people.

But it was his hair that truly amazed him. The careful work of the women had created something that was both utterly African and somehow Japanese as well—a perfect symbol of the cultural fusion that his entire life had become. He raised his hands to touch the carefully crafted sections, marveling at how something so practical could also be so beautiful.

Near the bath, he found a silk robe hanging from a wooden stand. Even at first glance, he could see that it was a garment of exceptional quality, the fabric shimmering with subtle patterns that seemed to shift in the light. When he put it on, however, the limitations of his size became immediately apparent. What should have been a full-length black and gold robe barely reached his knees, though the quality of the silk and the obvious care with which it had been tailored made it clear that this was the finest garment he had worn in years.

Feeling refreshed and strangely renewed, Majok moved toward the door of his quarters. But as he reached for the handle, he became aware of voices outside—guards, speaking in low tones that suggested they were there to ensure he remained where he had been placed.

The realization hit him like cold water. Despite the care he had been shown, despite the removal of his chains and the obvious expense invested in his preparation, he remained a prisoner. The beautiful room, the careful grooming, the silk robe—all of it was simply preparation for whatever use Nobunaga intended to make of him.

His eyes lowered instinctively to the ivory elephant around his neck, as the weight of it's existence grew heavier against his chest. The brief sense of peace and renewal began to fade, replaced by the hard reality of his situation.

"If they want to play their games, fine," he whispered to himself, his voice carrying a mixture of resignation and determination. "They can have their ceremonies and their preparations. But in the end, I will find my way back to what matters. Until then, I will survive whatever they require of me."

The words felt like both a promise and a threat, though he was not entirely certain to whom either was directed.

Chapter 9: The Mitingu

Dawn came to Azuchi-jo with the gentle sound of temple bells echoing across the compound, their bronze voices carrying the weight of centuries of tradition. Majok had been awake for some time, lying on his tatami mat and listening to the gradual awakening of the world around him—the soft footsteps of servants beginning their daily routines, the distant sounds of horses being tended in the stables, the quiet conversations of guards changing shifts.

The tranquility was shattered by the sound of his door sliding open with unnecessary force, followed by heavy footsteps and a voice that carried the particular edge of someone who enjoyed wielding authority over others.

"**Wake this inu up**!" Akechi's voice cut through the morning air like a blade. "**This dog isn't here to lie down and live off the land**."

Majok opened his eyes to see Akechi standing in the doorway, his elaborate armor catching the early light streaming through the translucent walls. Disoriented, Majok jumped to his feet and reflexively attempted to take a swing in the direction of Akechi to defend himself from what he considered aggressive behavior. But Akechi was much faster than the African—a testament to years of service as a skilled, seasoned General under the service of Nobunaga— and quickly sidestepped Majok and parried his attack, utilizing his sheathed sword as a weapon, and pummeling Majok to the floor. Akechi spun and pouned on Majok with cat-like reflexes before Majok could get his bearing, still bracing himself in a half-kneeled position. The next attack from Akechi this time was not a counter, but a full on swing as he slammed his sheathed weapon once again to the back of Majok. The sound of the air being sliced by the sword sent a shrill through over Majok's body that abruptly ceased when the weapon into him and crashed him into the floor. Majok tried to rolled sideways in an attempt to gain some foothold on the situation and turn the tables, but again, Akechi was too fast and used his leverage to pin Majok down with his knee on Majok's opposite shoulder while he connected three powerful punches that made the room spin before Majok's gaze. Majok's body went limp as his head slid to the wooden floor leaving him semi-conscious.

Satisfied by his handiwork, Akechi stood and holstered his weapon. He cackled as he turned to Ostrimyo who stood in the doorway. "**This inu is big, but no match for a fiery warrior such as myself. We will whip him into submission soon enough. He should consider himself grateful that he is not worthy of my blade. Get him up and prepared for a full day's labor**. "

Ostrimyo, his scarred face bearing an expression of patient resignation that suggested this was not an unusual way for the general to begin his day. Ostrimyo's translation, when it came, bore little resemblance to Akechi's harsh words. "Good morning, Majok-san," the old man said in English, his tone gentle despite the circumstances. "It's time to start our day."

Majok roused from his daze and slowly rolled to his side and sat up to face Ostrimyo, his movements sluggish but fluid despite the abrupt assault. As he stood, Akechi immediately began barking another series of commands, gesturing sharply toward the floor.

"**Tell him he must bow every time he sees me**!" Akechi demanded. "**I am his superior in every way, and he will show the proper respect**!"

Again, Ostrimyo's translation softened the general's harsh demands. "It is courteous to bow before high-ranking officials," he explained to Majok. "This is General Akechi, one of Lord Nobunaga's most trusted commanders. He is an esteemed member of the army and although he highly formidable with his sword, some consider him the best boy and arrow marksman this side of the orient. Please, offer him the appropriate respect."

Majok studied Akechi's face for a moment, reading the petty satisfaction there, then performed a respectful bow. The gesture seemed to please the general, though his expression remained cold and calculating.

"**Tell this inu that he belongs to me now**," Akechi continued, his voice taking on an increasingly unpleasant tone. "**He is only here because I requested him for my entertainment. He will consort with the other inus—ha! The dog pack!—and they will do my bidding like the animals they are**."

Ostrimyo paused for a moment, clearly choosing his words carefully. "On behalf of Lord Nobunaga, we welcome you to Azuchi-jo," he said finally. "The day is early, and we ask that you get dressed and join us for your orientation to the compound and some of the duties you will be assigned. Firstly, you will oversee the other five slaves and serve as their..." He paused, searching for an appropriate term.

"Slave driver?" Majok asked, his voice carrying a note of resignation.

Ostrimyo snapped his fingers as the right word came to him. "Coordinator. Yes, you will receive orders for assignments to be carried out each day and delegate who will do what, coordinating their efforts for maximum efficiency. Everyone will benefit. This is a new initiative that Lord Nobunaga is embarking upon and would appreciate your guidance."

Majok felt a familiar weight settling in his chest. "I don't think it works like that," he said quietly. "The other slaves will resent me for being elevated above them."

Before Ostrimyo could respond, Akechi barked out another command, his face twisted with cruel amusement. "**Tell him that like a good dog, he will lap at my feet whenever I command it, or he will face the ultimate penalty of death**!"

Ostrimyo's translation was far different to the threat that had just been issued. "Here, you will be considered the right-hand man to General Akechi. However, on the grounds, you and the other slaves will be regarded as... second-class citizens compared to all Japanese, as the general does not yet consider you his equal. At least, not yet. That status would have to be earned through demonstrated loyalty and competence."

Akechi then turned to Ostrimyo and spoke rapidly in Japanese, his tone suggesting he was giving specific instructions. When he finished, he strode from the room without another glance at Majok, leaving behind an atmosphere of tension and barely contained hostility.

"What did he say?" Majok asked.

"He wants you to tour the compound with one of the farm hands, to understand the layout of the land where you'll be working," Ostrimyo replied. "The young man should be here shortly."

As if summoned by their conversation, the door slid open to reveal a young Japanese man in his early twenties. Despite his simple clothing, there was something alert and intelligent in his eyes that suggested he was far more than just a laborer. When he spoke, his English was clear and unaccented. "Hello, Majok-san. I am Takeshi, though my friends call me Sunanomi."

"Good," Majok replied with genuine relief. "Someone else who speaks English."

"Yes, it is required of those who work in trade," Sunanomi explained. "So many foreigners travel our lands, and it is quite often that I have to conduct business with them. Only nobles maintain the privilege of speaking only Japanese. That is, with the exception of one."

"Who is that?" Majok asked.

The young man's eyes widened, then softened in a way that suggested his feelings about this person extended far beyond mere respect. "Oda Nobutada, the lord's son. He is a great warrior, but he also understands that knowledge of other languages is a tool of power." There was something in Sunanomi's tone—a note of admiration that bordered on affection—that made Majok study the young man's face more carefully.

"Sunanomi," Majok said after a moment. "Sand flea? If my friends called me that, I'd make new friends."

The young man laughed, his entire demeanor brightening. "On the contrary, Majok-san, I welcome the name. Lord Nobunaga bestowed it upon me himself. Something earned is always better than something given."

As they prepared to leave the dojo, Sunanomi kept stealing glances at Majok's imposing frame, his amazement clearly growing with each look. "Perhaps Lord Nobunaga will give you a great name one day as well," he said.

"It better not be anything smaller than a flea," Majok replied dryly.

"Oh, I'm sure it will be much larger than that!" Sunanomi's voice carried a weight of joy that reflected the abrupt fondness he had developed for his new companion. "Maybe something like Mount Kita or Yari, or even Hakusan. Or bigger yet—Mount Fuji!"

Ostrimyo, who had been listening to their exchange with interest, nodded his agreement. "Your size alone commands attention, Majok-san. But I suspect that in time, your other qualities may prove even more remarkable. Perhaps one day you might even join Lord Nobunaga's army proper."

The suggestion hung in the air like an impossible dream as they made their way out of the dojo. Majok changed from his sleeping robes into the simple sackcloth garments that had been provided for daily work—rough fabric that marked his station as clearly as if it had been written across his chest.

The tour of the compound revealed the full scope of Nobunaga's domain. Sunanomi proved to be an excellent guide, explaining not just the physical layout but the social and economic systems that kept everything functioning. They visited the stables where the finest horses in central Japan were bred and trained, the armories where weapons were forged and maintained, as well as the administrative buildings where the business of governing a province was conducted.

Finally, they arrived at the slave quarters—a cluster of buildings that, while functional rather than elegant, were maintained to standards that surprised Majok. Here he met the five people who would theoretically be under his supervision: three men and two women whose faces bore the particular expression of those who had learned to expect little and trust less.

After the initially introductions, the oldest of the men, a weathered individual whose dark skin spoke of origins far from Japan, studied Majok with open suspicion. "I am from the Americas," he said in English that carried traces of Spanish influence. "Deep in the southern tip, where I was supposed to remain. But my master found more value in trading me, so I was taken by Spanish traders. They sold me in India, and now I end up here." He paused, his eyes never leaving Majok's face. "I didn't see nothing good come from any man handling slaves, not even our own skin. When they assign you to be a slaver, you just as bad as the rest of them."

Before Majok could formulate a response to this challenge, Ostrimyo's voice called from outside the building. "Majok-san, it is time to prepare for this afternoon's presentation." As they walked back toward his quarters, Ostrimyo explained what was expected. "You will meet Lord Nobunaga's family in a formal setting. This is a great honor, but also a test. They will be evaluating you, determining what role you might play in their household."

"And what should I expect from them?" Majok asked with somber expectation.

Ostrimyo was quiet for a moment. "They will likely be... reserved. Skeptical, even. Your skin, your size, your origins—all of these things are foreign to them. Do not expect warmth initially. But if you prove yourself worthy of their trust, that may change in time."

Later That Afternoon

When Majok emerged from his quarters for the formal presentation, he had been transformed once again. The sackcloth of the morning had been replaced by garments that, while not approaching the magnificence of true nobility, spoke to care and respect. His robe was of good quality silk in deep brown, with subtle patterns that caught the light. Over it, he wore a haori jacket in darker brown that had been tailored to accommodate his impressive frame. The outfit was completed by hakama trousers that allowed for both dignity and movement.

The clothing struck the perfect balance—fine enough to show respect for the occasion and the family he was about to meet, but not so elaborate as to suggest he was attempting to rise above his station.

Akechi observed from a distance as Ostrimyo greeted Majok outside the main castle. The general had donned his finest armor for the occasion, the elaborate metalwork and silk cords creating an impression of barely contained violence wrapped in ceremony.

"Welcome, Majok-san," Ostrimyo said as they approached the castle's main entrance. "The family awaits in the Ōzashiki—the Grand Reception Hall."

The hall itself was a masterwork of Japanese architecture and design. Tall pillars supported a ceiling that seemed to soar toward the heavens, while silk banners bearing the Oda clan mon created splashes of color against the warm wood of the walls. At the far end of the hall, elevated on a dais that left no doubt about his authority, sat Oda Nobunaga.

The lord of Azuchi-jo was dressed in robes that seemed to capture light and hold it—silk so fine it appeared to move with its own wind, in shades of deep green and brilliant blue that spoke to wealth beyond imagination. His wife sat to his right, her own robes a symphony of colors and patterns that suggested both artistic sensibility and political power. To Nobunaga's left stood a young man who could only be his son, Nobutada, whose bearing suggested the confidence of someone raised to command.

"I will do most of the speaking initially," Ostrimyo explained in a low voice as they approached. "It is customary for introductions to be made in Japanese. You need not understand everything that is said—simply follow my lead."

What followed was a formal ceremony of introduction that felt both ancient and precisely choreographed. Ostrimyo's voice took on the cadences of court language as he presented Majok to the assembled family. "**I have the honor to present to the noble house of Oda: Nobunaga of the Oda Clan, Daimyo of Owari Province, Tenka-dono, Dairokuten Maō, Udaijin of the realm**." He gestured toward Nobunaga's wife. "**The honorable Lady Nōhime, whose wisdom guides the household**." Finally, his hand moved toward the young man. "**The valiant Oda Nobutada, heir to this great house and commander of armies**." He then turned toward Majok. "**And I present Majok, who comes to serve this household with loyalty and dedication**."

Ostrimyo motioned subtly, and Majok performed the deep bow he had been instructed in. Lady Nōhime offered a slight nod of acknowledgment, but Nobunaga remained completely motionless, his dark eyes fixed on Majok with an intensity that seemed to weigh and measure everything about him.

Lady Nōhime spoke, her voice carrying the musical quality of someone educated in the finest arts of speech.

Ostrimyo listened carefully, then turned to Majok. "The family graciously invites you to join them for the evening tea ceremony in their private chambers. This is a significant honor." Majok stared at him, unsure of how to received his words. "Smile and nod," Ostrimyo instructed quietly.

Majok did as directed, and Lady Nōhime's expression softened almost imperceptibly.

"Come this way," Ostrimyo said, leading him toward a smaller doorway that opened onto a more intimate space.

The tea chamber—the Chashitsu—was a study in refined simplicity. Every element had been chosen and placed with exquisite care, from the hanging scroll that provided the room's only decoration to the arrangement of flowers that seemed to capture the essence of the season. Low tables were arranged around the room, with cushions positioned to encourage both conversation and contemplation.

As they settled into the space, Ostrimyo took the opportunity to provide Majok with additional context about their host. "Lord Nobunaga has achieved remarkable things as ruler of Owari Province," he said quietly. "He implemented free markets by abolishing the old monopolies that strangled trade. He standardized weights, measures, and currency throughout his territories, making commerce more efficient. He conducted comprehensive land surveys to improve taxation and ensure fairness. And he disarmed the peasantry to prevent uprisings—what some call his 'Sword Hunt' edicts."

"He sounds like a man who understands both war and peace," Majok observed.

"Indeed. His mind works on levels that many cannot appreciate."

It was then that Nobutada approached them, moving with the casual confidence of someone completely comfortable in his own skin. When he spoke, his English was not just fluent but carried the slight accent of someone who had spent considerable time with foreign teachers. "So you're the giant everyone's been talking about," he said with a grin that was both friendly and slightly mischievous. "Quite impressive, I must say. You should do well as an overseer—though I suspect you're capable of much more than just watching over people."

His demeanor was immediately engaging, though there was something almost theatrical about his enthusiasm. As he continued speaking, it became clear that he was not immune to the kind of boastfulness that sometimes marked young men of high station.

"We've had our share of challenges here in Owari," he continued. "Revolts, uprisings, neighboring clans testing our resolve. But we've managed them all quite handily. My father's strategies are unmatched, and I've had the privilege of commanding armies in several successful campaigns. Soon, all the surrounding provinces will understand that resistance to the Oda clan is futile." He turned to Ostrimyo. "Wing, surely this man is destined for more than just coordinating the work of others? Someone of his obvious capabilities could contribute in many ways."

"Indeed," Ostrimyo replied carefully. "I'm sure we will find many things for Majok-san to do beyond baby sitting, especially when they can manage themselves. I suspect he is far more talented than such simple tasks would suggest."

Throughout the conversation, Majok was aware of Lord Nobunaga watching from across the room. The daimyo's wife engaged in quiet conversation with other family members, but Nobunaga himself remained largely silent, his attention frequently returning to assess this new addition to his household.

The tea ceremony itself was an education in Japanese refinement. Ostrimyo guided Majok through the various teas being served, explaining their origins and characteristics, suggesting which ones might appeal to his taste. The ritual aspects of the service—the precise movements, the careful attention to temperature and timing, the way each cup was presented—spoke to a culture that found profound meaning in the perfection of simple acts.

For nearly an hour, the gathering maintained its tone of restrained civility. Majok found himself relaxing slightly, beginning to appreciate both the ceremony and the company. Nobutada proved to be an engaging conversationalist, asking thoughtful questions about Majok's travels and experiences while sharing stories of his own military campaigns.

It was precisely at this moment of growing comfort that disaster struck.

Akechi, who had been moving around the periphery of the gathering, suddenly lurched forward as if stumbling. His shoulder struck Majok's arm just as the larger man was raising his tea cup, sending the delicate porcelain flying from his grasp to shatter against the polished wooden floor.

"**Clumsy inu**!" Akechi barked immediately, his voice carrying clearly across the now-silent room. "**Look what you've done! Clean up after yourself!**"

He gestured sharply toward a servant girl, who immediately produced a cloth towel. But instead of handing it to Majok, Akechi tossed it toward Ostrimyo, who, being blind, could not see the projectile coming and missed it entirely.

"**Tell this dog to clean up the mess he's made**!" Akechi commanded, his voice full of cruel satisfaction.

Nobutada immediately stepped forward, his face flushing with anger. "**General Akechi, your behavior is inappropriate for this setting. The collision was clearly accidental**."

But Majok had already recognized the true nature of what was happening. Without a word, he bent down and retrieved the towel from where it had fallen near Ostrimyo's feet, then began carefully cleaning up the spilled tea and gathering the fragments of broken porcelain.

Akechi watched this display with obvious delight, then deliberately poured the remaining tea from his own cup onto the floor directly in front of Majok.

"**Inu, you missed a spot**," he said with a laugh that held no humor whatsoever.

Majok felt rage building in his chest like a fire being fed fresh kindling. His hands, engaged in cleaning up the mess, began to tremble slightly as he fought to control the fury that threatened to overwhelm his judgment. The ivory elephant around his neck seemed to grow heavier, a reminder of what he stood to lose if he gave in to his anger.

Akechi noticed the change in Majok's demeanor and his eyes lit up with anticipation. In one fluid motion, he drew his katana from its scabbard and held it with both hands above Majok's neck, the steel catching the light from the room's lamps. A chorus of gasps filled the chamber. "**Try it**," he said in Japanese, his voice carrying deadly invitation. "**I implore you to give me a reason**."

The tension in the room became almost unbearable. Every person present understood that they were witnessing a moment that could end in blood and death, with consequences that would ripple far beyond this single evening.

It was Nobunaga's voice that cut through the silence like a blade of its own. "**Akechi**!" The daimyo's shout echoed off the walls of the chamber, carrying an authority that made even the general freeze. "**That is enough! You dishonor this ceremony, our guest, and therefore me. Your duty here is finished. You are dismissed**!"

The command left no room for argument or discussion. Akechi slowly sheathed his sword, but the smile on his face as he bowed and departed suggested that he considered the evening a victory rather than a defeat.

When the general had gone, the tea chamber felt somehow larger, as if a poisonous presence had been extracted from the air. Nobutada immediately moved toward Majok, extending his hand to help him rise from where he knelt on the floor.

But Majok ignored the offered assistance, instead turning toward Ostrimyo. "Am I permitted to leave now?" he asked quietly.

Ostrimyo nodded, his scarred face showing both understanding and regret. "You may."

As Majok rose to his full height and prepared to depart, his eyes met Nobunaga's one final time across the room. The daimyo's expression was unreadable, but there was something in his gaze—a measuring quality that suggested the evening's events had revealed more about all the participants than anyone might have expected.

Without another word, Majok bowed formally to the assembled family and departed, leaving behind a tea ceremony that would be remembered not for its ritual elegance, but for the glimpse it had provided into the complex and dangerous dynamics that governed life within the walls of Azuchi-jo.

Chapter 10: The Mwali

The dawn mist clung to the rice fields as Majok emerged from the slave quarters, his tall frame silhouetted against the lightening sky. Weeks had turned to months since his arrival at Azuchi-jo, and he had settled into the rhythm of overseeing the compound's expanding agricultural operations.

Under Ostrimyo's direction, Majok had been given authority over the other five slaves—a mix of captured farmers and displaced peasants who had found themselves bound to Nobunaga's service. His days began before sunrise: directing the tilling of new fields, organizing the cleaning of farm houses, and supervising repairs to the compound's aging walls where winter storms had taken their toll.

But two primary tasks dominated his responsibilities, both assigned directly by Ostrimyo with Lord Nobunaga's blessing.

The first was the construction of a protective wooden fence along Azuchi-jo's southern border. Wild boars had been ravaging the rice fields with increasing boldness, and the compound's livestock—essential for maintaining self-sufficiency—needed better protection in their farm sheds. "The beasts grow bolder each season," Ostrimyo explained as they walked the proposed fence line one morning. "But it's not only the animals we must consider, Majok-san." Majok shot him a perplexed look. The older man's voice dropped to a more serious tone. "Our people believe that evil spirits dwell in the land beyond these plains, deep in the darker forests. The fence serves a dual purpose—keeping the physical threats out while providing spiritual protection for our people."

Majok nodded respectfully, though privately he thought of his own homeland's beliefs about protective barriers. Every culture, it seemed, understood the wisdom of walls against both seen and unseen dangers.

The second major task was tending to Nobunaga's ambitious wine vineyard project. The year-old vines represented their lord's fascination with foreign customs and Eastern philosophies—an experiment that had raised eyebrows throughout the compound. And although his new interest in having slaves under his service was a representation of that as well, the vines became his most prized obsession. "Lord Nobunaga believes that mastering foreign arts will strengthen Japan," Ostrimyo had explained. "Wine-making, slave labor—these are tools he wishes to understand and control."

Not everyone shared this enthusiasm. Majok had overheard a heated conversation between Ostrimyo and Akechi Mitsuhide near the administrative buildings, Akechi's voice tight with disapproval.

"These foreign influences corrupt traditional values," Akechi had argued. "Slaves, wine-making, exotic philosophies—where does it end, Ostrimyo-san? We risk losing what makes us Japanese."

Ostrimyo's reply had been diplomatic but firm. "Lord Nobunaga's vision extends beyond our borders. He sees strength in adaptation."

"I see weakness in abandonment of our ways," Akechi had countered before storming away, his hand resting on his sword hilt—a gesture that had become increasingly common.

Now, months later, as Majok supervised the daily operations, he could feel the weight of these cultural tensions in every interaction. The vineyard struggled despite a full year of attention, and questions were beginning to surface about the wisdom of the entire enterprise.

It was during one of his morning inspections that the crisis came to a head. The morning sun cast long shadows across the compound as he examined the struggling vineyard alongside Ostrimyo. "The young lord grows impatient," Ostrimyo said, his weathered hands gesturing toward the wilting vines. "Nobutada-sama believes more water will solve the problem. He wants the slaves to irrigate the land further and add new channels next to the vines."

"The slaves? I'm not sure they'll be of much assistance. Their motivation to do anything I ask had worn with each request. I fear that their hatred of me grows more each hour. "

"Oh? Why is that?" Ostrimyo asked.

"They see me as part of their oppression and less as a supervision or *Coordinator* as you all see it," Majok replied.

"Give them time, Majok-san. Like the melting of the ice on the mountain tops as the season of spring ushers along, change is a necessary evil that calls for acceptance. The adjustment is never easy, but the adaptation to the new found set of circumstances that it brings with it also carries opportunities that sometimes are not yet seen, initially," Ostrimyo added. "In time, they will come both honor and respect you. Trust the process."

Majok's attention turned back to the vineyards. He studied the drooping leaves, his Dinka farming instincts immediately recognizing the issue. "With respect, Ostrimyo-san, may I offer a counter suggestion?"

The older man's eyebrows rose with curiosity. "You may."

"These vines are dying not from lack of water, but from too much of it," Majok explained, his voice carrying subtle enthusiasm. "In my homeland, we learned that certain crops must be challenged to thrive. These lands are too wet—the vines have become lazy, their roots shallow. Adding more irrigation would be a grave mistake."

Ostrimyo considered the words carefully, his experienced gaze moving from the struggling plants to the determined expression on Majok's dark features. "I will discuss this with Nobutada-sama, but I see wisdom in your words. Proceed with your assessment while I address him."

The next morning, Ostrimyo returned to Majok's quarters accompanied by Sunanomi, whose presence always seemed to brighten when the young African was near.

"After much conversation with Nobutada-sama," Ostrimyo announced, "your request has been granted. We have permission to begin transplanting the vines to higher, drier ground as a test."

"Nobutada-sama is young, but wise beyond his years. I am pleased that you found favor in his eyes. It will be an honor to work alongside you, Majok-san," Sunanomi said with a polite bow, though the crimson flush spreading across his cheeks betrayed emotions beyond mere professional courtesy.

Majok noticed the telltale blush but held his tongue, not wanting to embarrass the young man in front of Ostrimyo. "We must work swiftly," he said instead. "I'd hate to lose any crops this season. The vines need to be stressed by fighting for water—it will make them stronger, more robust. They should sell for double on the market."

"Brilliant, Majok-san," Sunanomi replied, his boyish grin impossible to contain. "Nobutada-sama instructed us to try this approach with one quarter of the crop this fall season, and then evaluate the results come spring."

"He spoke directly to you?" Majok asked, surprised.

"Yes, Majok-san," Sunanomi confirmed, his smile widening at the memory of the interaction.

"Very well," Majok replied flatly, though inwardly he felt a flicker of satisfaction at having his agricultural knowledge recognized.

The autumn air carried the sweet scent of ripening grapes as Majok walked through the vineyard rows months later, his practiced eye assessing the heavy clusters. Three seasons had passed since he'd first suggested the terraced planting, and now the evidence of his Dinka agricultural wisdom hung abundantly before them.

Over this time, Majok was also pleased that some scheduling restrictions had been lifted from him, which allowed time to be spent for personal desires. So he dedicated parts of his day to deep meditation, prayer, and exercise. Since Japanese culture was not heavily influenced by basic weight lifting, there was nothing for him to use other than his own body weight to build his muscles. Push-ups, pull-ups, dips, lunges and squats became a regimen to sink his teeth into and fulfill his appetite to stay fit. He also spent some time in the evenings practicing various katas from his African martial arts. More than a few times, his actions caught the attention of the townsfolk of Azuchi-jo and apparently young Nobutada, as Majok caught him observing several times from the safety of his balcony on the palace. A sense of pride washed over Majok as he trained, hopeful that the traditions and practices of this foreigner would rub off on the native eyes around him.

But it was the harvest that made his chest poke out the most. It had exceeded all expectations, and word of the vineyard's success had reached the main compound by midday. Ostrimyo found Majok among the vines, his weathered face creased with satisfaction.

"Majok-san," he called, approaching with measured steps. "Lord Nobunaga has called for a formal assessment. The retainers are gathering in the great hall to review the agricultural reports."

The great hall of Azuchi-jo was an imposing space, its high wooden beams casting long shadows across the polished floors. At just the right angle, the blinding light reflected from the sun could stab at your eyes with near razor-like sharpness. Sliding panels had been drawn back to reveal the autumn landscape beyond, while braziers provided warmth against the cooling air. The assembled retainers sat in formal rows, their silk robes a rainbow of rank and status, each man positioned according to his standing within Nobunaga's hierarchy.

At the head of the room, Nobunaga occupied his elevated platform, sake cup in hand, his sharp eyes taking in every detail of the proceedings. To his right sat Nobutada, while the various magistrates and administrators arranged themselves in careful order of precedence.

Majok entered quietly, taking his designated position near the back alongside the other household servants and supervisors. From there, he could observe the formal presentation of the season's achievements.

"**Twenty percent increase in yield**," Watanabe Jinzaemon announced to the assembled retainers, his voice carrying the satisfaction of a man whose ledgers told a profitable story. The Kanjo-bugyō's silk robes rustled as he gestured toward the vineyard visible through the open panels. "**Both from direct grape sales and our wine production**."

Nobunaga nodded approvingly from his elevated position, sake cup in hand. "**Excellent results**."

But Akechi Mitsuhide's jaw tightened, his hands clenching at his sides. "My lord, might I question these numbers? Such dramatic improvement seems... unlikely."

"Are you suggesting our Finance Magistrate cannot count?" Nobunaga's tone carried a dangerous edge.

Akechi's voice grew bolder. "Of course not, my lord. I merely wonder about the circumstances. More concerning is that such a significant decision—relocating the vineyard—was made without your knowledge or approval."

The room fell silent. Nobunaga's eyes narrowed as he turned to his son. "Nobutada?"

"The initiative was mine, Father," Nobutada replied steadily. "But I cannot take all the credit. The agricultural wisdom came from Majok-san, the Coordinator."

Everyone's attention turned Majok as the room came to an abrupt hush. His heart riveted in his chest, as even though he had begun to understand some basic words of Japanese dialect, the speed at which this conversation proceeded left him ill-prepared to digest the subject mater. All he knew was that he was now the focus of their discussion.

Akechi shot to his feet, his voice rising. "Now the heir to the Oda clan takes orders from an inu! This is nepotism at its worst, Lord Nobunaga. It will dilute our clan's respect. Surrounding clans will get wind of this—may already have. You'll lose what waning respect you still command."

The words hung in the air like poison. Nobunaga rose slowly, his presence filling the room with menace. "Not unlike your family, Akechi," Nobunaga said, his voice deadly quiet. "As I recall, it was my hand that salvaged your family's name. If it wasn't for me, Lady Saitō would still be considered the harlot that was paraded around the Takeda territories during your... formative years."

Akechi's face went white, then flushed crimson with rage. "How dare you—"

"I am daimyo!" Nobunaga roared, rising to his feet. "I do as I desire!"

Akechi bowed stiffly, retaking his seat. "As you desire, Lord," he grunted through gritted teeth.

Nobunaga's demeanor shifted like a weather vane. "Well done, Nobutada. Where did you acquire such brilliant insight?"

"I cannot take all the credit, Father. The suggestion to move the vines to higher, dryer grounds came from Majok-san, the Coordinator."

As Akechi began to rise again, clearly unable to contain his disgust, Nobunaga's voice cut through the air. "It is considered a great insult to leave a meeting without being dismissed, Akechi. Some would even consider it treachery. Would you like me to strike it from the record?"

"May I leave, *great* daimyo?" Akechi asked, his voice barely controlled.

Nobunaga turned to his son with theatrical deliberation. "Nobutada has the floor. Nobutada, is he dismissed?"

"Dismissed, *great* warrior," Nobutada replied.

Akechi exited with a perfunctory bow and stormed from the hall.

Nobunaga looked upon his son with newfound interest. He leaned in to speak with him in privately. "See to it that you keep me informed of such decisions in the future. And update me on any further interactions with this... Coordinator."

"Yes, Father."

Three Weeks Later

The rhythmic clacking of wooden swords echoed through the dojo as Majok and Nobutada circled each other in what had become their secret training sessions. What had begun as a chance encounter—Nobutada practicing alone in the courtyard after his regular partner had been injured, inviting the tall African to help—had blossomed into mutual respect and genuine friendship.

Nobutada identified that Majok possessed all the stature and skill to pose as a formidable opponent for training and inquired with Ostrimyo if the idea made sense. To his surprise, the Wing had no objections to Nobutada's request, agreeing with him so succinctly that Nobutada was convinced that it was an idea Ostrimyo had already considered himself.

They had been careful to train when others were occupied with their duties, keeping their sessions private. Ostrimyo supervised from the sidelines, being the only one privy to their arrangement. His weathered face showed approval as he observed the two—relying on sound and vibration in the absence of sight—to judge and offer correction to form and fighting styles as the two young men exchanged techniques. Majok's African martial arts blended surprisingly well with Japanese sword work, each teaching the other, each learning. The only thing Majok requested in exchange for the trainings was that Nobutada taught him Japanese. Being ignorant to conversations and dialogue—much of which Majok was sure pertained to him—was frustrating to say the least. Besides, if he was to be here for the unseen future, he might as well settle in and learn as much as possible to make himself comfortable.

"Good, good. Now reset Majok and hold your blocking arm higher next time. Don't make it so easy for Nobutada-sama to engage with his striking hand," Ostrimyo barked from the sideline.

Majok straightened, dropped his back foot, held his defensive stance. "Yes, sir," he said as he turned his attention back to Nobutada. "Honestly, I don't know how he's doing that," Majok said.

Nobutada chuckled. "Neither do I, but after so many years, you learn to just accept it and obey. He is more than a teacher; he is the ears of the compound. No one can attack us without him knowing as he relies on the wind to bring him information. The sound of troops marching, horses galloping, and even weapons being loaded—all the sounds of war. None of which is ever invisible to his sensitive ears."

"Speaking of which," Ostrimyo began, "I can hear you growing sloppy, so you'd do well to adjust the timing of your attack Nobutada-sama. The strongest attack is a straight one. The sound of the air betrays your—"

"Slow approach! I get it Wing," Nobutada replied, frustration in his tone.

"Don't look at me like that, young man, I've only been training you since you entered this world," Ostrimyo said as he adjusted in his seat, the wooden chair pressing into the floor, creaking to the tune of his frustration.

Just then the dojo doors slid open with a sharp crack.

Instantly, Ostrimyo barked something aloud. Majok couldn't quite make out what it meant, but judging by Nobuatada's prompt response—him dropping the wooden weapon in his hands and facing the door, head dropped slightly while maintaining a firm eye gaze—he could only imagine it was expedient that he follow suit.

And so he did.

To his dismay, Nobunaga stepped through, accompanied by three samurai retainers. Majok and Nobutada dropped to their knees, bowing deeply, both fearing the worst about their unauthorized sessions.

"**What is going on here**?" Nobunaga asked, his voice unreadable.

Ostrimyo rose and stepped forward quickly. "**My lord, Nobutada-sama has been training with Majok-san. It began when the young lord's usual partner was injured. Majok-san proved... surprisingly skilled in combat arts from his homeland. They have been exchanging techniques**."

Nobunaga remained silent, his sharp eyes taking in every detail—the wooden swords, the sweat on both men's brows, the easy camaraderie that had clearly developed between them, the obvious secrecy of their arrangement.

The silence stretched until it became unbearable.

Finally, Nobunaga turned toward the door. He called to his guards, and the doors slid open again. He paused, looking back at his son with a solemn, unreadable stare.

Then he left without a word.

One Week Later

"You will train with them," Nobunaga announced to Akechi in his private chambers. "I am ordering formal training sessions. You, Nobutada, and the African will train together."

Akechi's face contorted with barely suppressed rage. "My lord, I must protest—"

"You must do nothing but obey," Nobunaga cut him off. "Unless you question my authority?"

"Many of the men are losing respect for you," Akechi said, his voice low and dangerous. "Teaching our techniques to an outsider... they whisper that you should banish him. When soldiers lose morale, they will not fight as well. More forces rally against us daily because of decisions like this."

Nobunaga stepped closer, his voice dropping to a whisper. "I am daimyo, and I do as I please. Not as the people demand. You will train with them, and anyone who even whispers of their disregard for my authority will be killed."

"Your judgment is clouded by your emotions regarding your son," Akechi replied, his composure finally cracking. "You must end this madness before it destroys us all."

"You have your orders. Carry them out."

The Following Week

But Akechi had already decided on a different course of action. Rather than training himself, he assigned another soldier to take his place, claiming pressing administrative duties that required his attention.

When word reached Nobunaga of Akechi's defiance, the confrontation was swift and brutal. "You were given a direct order," Nobunaga snarled, cornering Akechi in the administrative quarters. "Explain your disobedience."

"I assigned Sergeant Hayashi to represent me," Akechi replied stiffly. "My duties as—"

"Your duties are what I say they are. Resume your training immediately, or face the consequences of insubordination."

Akechi's jaw tightened, but he had no choice. "As you command, my lord."

Two Days Later

The wooden swords clacked together in the dojo as Majok and Nobutada sparred, their movements fluid and practiced. Neither noticed when Akechi entered, nor when Nobunaga himself slipped in to observe from the shadows.

Akechi joined the bout, taking the opportunity to attempt to humiliate the African who had somehow gained such favor. The fight intensified, wooden blades moved faster, and strikes became harder.

Majok's superior reach and unorthodox techniques began to take their toll on Akechi and before long, fatigue began to set it. In true expectation, the daily callisthenic training of Majok proved superior that of the General's, allowing him to slide in between wild swings to strike Akechi with precise blows that slowly wore him down. Akechi's rage began to worm its way in now, mixing well with his pride making him even more susceptible to Majok's attacks. It wasn't until Akechi noticed Nobuatada sporting a smirk that he lost control and succumbed to Majok's final exchange that left him disarmed. The wooden sword rattled along the floor, shaking away the last ounce of Akechi's dignity.

The defeat was more than Akechi could bear. His hand moved to his real sword, the steel singing as it left its scabbard. With a roar of rage, he rushed at Majok, the blade aimed at the African's throat.

But Majok didn't raise his guard. Instead, he stood perfectly still, his hand moving unconsciously to touch the elephant-tusk necklace beneath his clothing. The months of separation from his family, the constant tension, the knowledge that he was utterly alone in this foreign land—it all crystallized into a moment of devastating acceptance.

"I welcome death," he whispered in Dinka.

Just as Akechi's blade would have found its mark, Nobunaga's sword thrust between them, the steel ringing as it blocked the strike.

"**Akechi**," Nobunaga said in Japanese, his voice deadly calm, "**you would dishonor yourself and this domain by killing an unarmed warrior who is not fighting back**?"

Akechi replied in rapid, angry Japanese. "**This inu is no warrior! He is not worthy of any act of honor**." Though Majok couldn't understand the exchange, he could feel the murderous intent radiating from Akechi's every word.

"I *can* and *will* determine the honor of anyone in this land!" Nobunaga hissed.

But Akechi knew that Nobunaga's response was sharp and final. The look in his eyes spoke higher volume than any of the Demon King of the Sixth Heaven's words. So, Akechi sheathed his sword with a snap and stalked from the dojo, but not before turning back to deliver what sounded like a warning or threat in Japanese, his burning eyes fixed on Majok all the while. "**I will do only what is necessary to maintain honor within this clan**."

Majok was crowned the mwali—victor in Dinka. Majok took in a deep, slow breath as the elephant tusk that represented his identity, his heritage, and his very soul—pressed against his chest like a promise. Or perhaps like a warning of the fire that was coming to consume them all.

Chapter 11: The Shokubai

Weeks Later – Late 1580

The soft scratch of brush against rice paper filled the quiet corner of the training ground where Nobutada and Majok sat cross-legged, a collection of practice sheets spread between them. The young lord's careful strokes formed the flowing characters of hiragana as he guided Majok through the intricacies of written Japanese.

"Bu-shi," Nobutada said slowly, pointing to the characters he'd just written. "Warrior." Majok studied the elegant curves, then attempted to copy them on his own sheet. His large hands, more accustomed to farm tools than brushes, produced slightly shaky but recognizable characters. "Very good," Nobutada encouraged. "Now try... uma. Horse."

"Fine," Majok replied, determined to do better.

As Majok practiced the new characters, Nobutada continued with other essential words: "Sake—rice wine. Tori—bird. Ishi—stone." Each word was carefully written and repeated until Majok could recognize and roughly reproduce them.

"You're a natural," Nobutada said after watching Majok successfully write several words from memory.

Majok looked up from his practice sheet, a slight smile playing at his lips. "When you've traveled to as many continents as I have, it becomes beneficial to understand many tongues in order to survive. It's less a luxury and more a necessity."

"How did you learn English so well?" Nobutada asked, genuine curiosity in his voice.

Majok tilted his head as if to shake free a memory from the past, one laced with equal parts pain and admiration. "My previous owner was a rich, well-traveled Englishman. He took great pride in his slaves and wanted them to speak eloquently when he showed us off to his compatriots. His wife was a teacher and took her time to correct and educate us at every turn when any of us spoke out of context. It was very difficult." He paused, setting down his brush. "Where I'm from, Dinka is the chosen language, and I find that although English is the popular tongue in the East, it has both too many rules and too many liberties. Slang, as they call it, confounds me quite often. So, I just prefer to do as they say—shoot straight with what I mean and say."

Nobutada shrugged, not fully comprehending everything Majok said, but appreciating it nonetheless. "Well, you do it quite well. And I agree with you that English is a bit of a chore."

"Likewise. You are quite impressive with your mastery also," Majok replied.

"Thank you, Majok-san," Nobutada said. There was a pause between them, and Majok could tell that the young lord had something weighing on his mind.

"What is it?" Majok asked.

"I'm sorry about your past... being separated from your family—not only as a child but also as a father. I could never have survived such a thing," Nobutada said softly.

Majok's expression grew thoughtful. "In time, you'll learn that the human mind is very pliable, like strong bamboo as it sways in the wind from a powerful storm. It can be stretched to levels you never imagine it could, only to rebound and return even stronger."

"Still, you have my respect and my word," Nobutada said earnestly. "When my father has finally brought unity to the Owari, and hopefully, one day, all of Japan as Emperor, we will find your family, and you will have your freedom. We will vanquish slavery on this continent and if I have my way, all across the globe."

Majok's eyes held a mixture of gratitude and skepticism. "Thank you. But I've seen the hearts of men. It is an unquenchable evil. I'm not sure that just one man can make a difference."

"I can, and I will. You'll see. As long as I'm around, no harm will come to you."

"Thank you, young lord," Majok said with a bow and a wide smile.

Nobutada paused, then spoke hesitantly, clearly struggling with words he couldn't bring himself to say. "Tomorrow, Majok-san, I..." Nobutada sighed as the words lingered on his tongue.

"Yes, Nobutada-sama. Go on."

"Well... I wanted to ask you... I mean, are you ever tired?"

"Tired hardly describes how I feel most days."

"Wars take a toll on you and after a while, I wish to just be home. Away from all the turmoil."

"With a family?"

"I don't know. Maybe... I guess. Father would want that."

"But what do you want? You're a man now. You need to make your own decisions about who you are and who you want to be."

"Maybe," Nobutada said, dropping his head. "Maybe you can show me how. My father is a strong-willed man and doesn't believe in people going against his will or the natural order of things."

Majok clapped his hand on Nobutada's shoulder, noting how the young lord's disposition had waned. "A father that truly loves his family will do what's best for them, even if it goes against his ideals. Trust his love—I know he holds it dearly for you."

The Next Morning

The training ground was shrouded in pre-dawn mist as Ostrimyo and Majok faced each other, wooden swords at the ready. The old retainer moved with a fluidity that belied his years, demonstrating the technique he called "Twin Blade."

"Blades of grass sway in the wind. You must be the same," Ostrimyo instructed, his movements flowing like water as he showed Majok how to respond fluidly to each swing and counter-movement. "Kenjutsu is not about overpowering your opponent—it is about becoming one with the rhythm of battle." Ostrimyo set his feet and readied his sword. "Now, try to attack me," Ostrimyo commanded as he dropped his back foot and raised his guard.

Majok raised a concerned brow. "But Wing, I can—"

"Afraid you will hurt a blind old man?" Ostrimyo asked, cutting him off.

"No, it's just—"

"Then attack me! Trust me, I will be fine. Any uncertainty in the field of battle will end in death. Only decisiveness can kill fear."

"But I will never be in battle. I am a mere slave... *Coordinator.*"

Ostrimyo dropped his guard and slowly closed the distance between them. He placed a tentative hand on Majok's chest, directly over his heart. "On the contrary. You may not be a warrior yet, but the blood of a warrior flows through your veins. It takes a strong heart to endure what you have endured. You, Majok-san, have a very strong heart. A man is only what he says he is—first in his heart and then in his mind."

Ostrimyo stepped back to re-open the space between them. This time, Majok set his feet to attack, determined to strike just hard enough to make a statement, but not to disable the old retainer. And so he did. As Majok attacked, Ostrimyo swayed from side to side and then backwards, dodging each swing and bending over backwards in a position that seemed impossible for anyone to hold, especially not someone of his elder years. As Majok gawked in amazement, Ostrimyo took the opportunity to parry his attack and send a leg sweep that toppled the large African.

Majok landed with a thud. Ostrimyo paused and dropped his sword to his side as he straightened his body. "Now, do you see?"

Majok stood and sighed. "Absolutely."

"Again," Ostrimyo said as he began to set his feet once more.

But just as they were about to resume sparring, the thunder of hooves filled the air. Akechi led a troop of mounted warriors through the compound, their armor gleaming in the morning light, banners snapping in the wind.

Majok stopped and regarded them. "Where are they going?" he asked Ostrimyo.

"To war," Ostrimyo replied solemnly.

As an endless sea of warriors rode by, Majok saw Nobutada bringing up the rear, his young face set with grim determination. The lord's son failed to make eye contact with Majok as he rode through the gates, and Majok felt a sense of anguish and fear that he might not return.

Days Later – Deep In the Night

The sound of approaching horses stirred the compound from sleep. Majok emerged from his quarters, his eyes desperately searching the returning troops for Nobutada's face. The warriors were celebrating victory—their triumphant voices carried news of another successful campaign against the Ikko-ikki rebels, the Buddhist militants who had been harassing the eastern borders for months.

When he finally spotted Nobutada, relief flooded through him, followed immediately by concern. The young lord was alive, but wounded, lying in a wagon with his torso wrapped in white bandages, his face pale but alert.

As Majok started to approach, Akechi's harsh voice cut through the night air, barking orders in rapid Japanese. Though Majok had learned much of the language, Akechi spoke too quickly and with too much military terminology for him to fully understand.

Akechi turned to Ostrimyo, speaking in clipped, authoritative Japanese, gesturing sharply toward the rear carriages and then at Majok. His tone carried the particular venom he reserved for giving orders about the African.

Ostrimyo listened with his usual patient expression before turning to Majok. "Akechi-sama commands that you take the other slaves and unload the carriages at the back of the convoy," he translated. "They contain our fallen warriors. The slaves are to strip the armor and prepare the bodies for proper funeral rites according to our customs. However, you are not to touch the bodies yourself—only supervise the others. He says he will have additional tasks for you once this work is completed."

Through The Night

As the hours passed, Majok supervised the grim work of preparing the fallen for their final rest. The slaves worked alongside other compound workers to remove armor and prepare the bodies according to Japanese custom—washing them with care, arranging them in proper positions, and beginning the ritual preparations that would honor their sacrifice.

But the work bred resentment. Majok could hear the whispered conversations growing bitterer as the night wore on. "Look at him," one of the male slaves muttered to another as they worked. "Standing there watching us do the real work while he gives orders like some lord."

"He thinks he's better than us now," the other replied. "Gets special treatment, eats better food, trains with the samurai. Forgets where he came from."

Majok heard their words and felt them cut deep. He approached the two men, his voice filled with pain. "We must stand united, brothers. Akechi seeks to divide us—can't you see that?"

The first slave looked up from his grim task, his eyes blazing with anger. "How can we stand united when you sit at a table that we are not even allowed to eat crumbs from?"

The words cut Majok to the bone, and he found himself without an answer.

Dawn

As the work neared completion, Akechi returned and summoned both Majok and Ostrimyo. Speaking only to the old retainer in rapid

Japanese once more, he issued new orders with sharp gestures toward the piles of recovered armor.

Ostrimyo turned to Majok. "Akechi-sama says you must now clean all this armor, by yourself."

"But this will take days to accomplish such a thing," Majok protested in English, understanding enough of what had been said to grasp the enormity of the task.

Akechi, not understanding Majok's English response, turned back to Ostrimyo with raised eyebrows, clearly demanding translation. Ostrimyo explained Majok's concern in Japanese.

Akechi's response was swift and dismissive as he continued speaking only to Ostrimyo, his gestures becoming more animated. When he finished, Ostrimyo turned back to Majok with a resigned expression. "He says he doesn't care if it takes years. All your other duties are officially suspended. The armor must be prepared properly. He's also calling for the blacksmiths to begin repairs, and you are to work alongside them and learn their craft as well." Ostrimyo paused, clearly reluctant to translate the final insult. "He says... if nothing else, you have proven that one can teach an old dog new tricks."

Days Later

Majok worked from dawn to dusk, learning the intricate art of maintaining samurai armor. Each piece told a story of the warrior who had worn it—the do chest plates with their layered scales, the kabuto helmets with their distinctive crests, the kote arm guards with their delicate mail work.

Under the patient guidance of the compound's blacksmiths, he learned to clean the lacquered surfaces without damaging them, to repair breaks in the silk cords that bound the plates together, and to understand the symbolic meaning of each component. The menpo face masks, he learned, were not just protection but spiritual armor, meant to strike fear into enemies while protecting the wearer's soul in battle.

"Each piece must be perfect," old Master Hayashi had explained as he showed Majok how to polish a tarnished helmet. "The armor is not just protection—it is the samurai's honor made manifest."

When the work was finally complete, Ostrimyo came to collect him. "Nobutada-sama has summoned you," he said simply.

They found the young lord in his recovery chambers, still pale but sitting upright, his wounds clearly healing well. His face lit up when he saw Majok enter. "Majok-san! I'm so glad to see you well."

"And I you, young lord. How do you feel?"

"Better each day. The campaign was successful—we finally crushed the Ikko-ikki resistance in the eastern territories. Father will be pleased that those rebel strongholds can no longer threaten our borders. But I'm glad to be home." Nobutada's expression grew more serious. "I heard about the work Akechi assigned you. I'm sorry I couldn't prevent it."

"It taught me much," Majok replied diplomatically. "I understand now the sacred nature of the samurai's equipment."

"That's... one way to look at it," Nobutada said with a weak smile.

The Next Evening

Rain drummed against the wooden panels of Nobunaga's private chambers as Ostrimyo led Majok into the presence of the daimyo. Majok prepared himself for another silent meeting with translation through Ostrimyo, but was stunned when Nobunaga looked up and spoke directly to him—in English.

"I summoned you here to talk about the crops," Nobunaga said, his accent thick but his words clear. "They are progressing well."

Majok's amazement at hearing Nobunaga speak English directly was evident on his face. "You speak the popular tongue?"

"Of course, I am not ignorant," Nobunaga replied with a slight smile.

"Yes, daimyo. The crops are doing quite well. I too have observed their progress," Majok said.

"As far as keeping my ability to speak English, I needed to be sure that you could be trusted before being addressed directly," Nobunaga explained. "So far, your hard work has earned that trust. My son has been... instructive... in teaching me your tongue."

"I am honored by your confidence, daimyo."

"But this does not assure your release anytime soon," Nobunaga continued, his tone becoming more serious. "It will take more time."

Majok's hands clenched at his sides as the hope of freedom was once again deferred, but he kept his voice steady. "Yes, daimyo, of course."

Suddenly, the night sky exploded with light. Lightning struck one of the slave quarters with supernatural intensity, and flames erupted immediately. The crack of thunder was followed by screams echoing in the distance, then an explosion that shook the ground beneath their feet.

Majok turned to Ostrimyo, trained by months of obedience not to act without permission. Before the old retainer could speak, Nobunaga commanded in English, "Quickly, go and help them!"

Majok ran from the chamber and across the compound toward the blazing slave quarters. The building was already half-consumed by flames that seemed to burn with unnatural intensity and color. Through the smoke and chaos, he could hear voices crying for help from within.

Without hesitation, he plunged into the inferno.

The heat was overwhelming, the smoke choking, but he pressed forward. In the back corner of the building, he found them—one of the young slave women, unconscious from smoke, and beside her a Japanese girl no more than ten years old who reminded him painfully of his own daughter. Both were trapped by fallen burning beams.

Using strength born of desperation, he lifted the beams and gathered both girls in his arms. The flames licked at his clothing as he carried them toward the exit, the roof beginning to collapse around them.

Majok emerged from the slave quarters with both girls safe in his arms, but his own clothing was ablaze. He set the girls down gently, then fell to the ground as the fire consumed his shirt and began to burn his flesh.

As if from out of nowhere, Nobutada appeared from behind the crowd of onlookers, a wet blanket in his hands. Despite his own injuries, he wrapped Majok in the blanket and rolled him on the ground until the flames were extinguished.

When the fire was out, Majok's charred body was revealed—angry welts of singed flesh covered his shoulders, chest, and back. The elephant tusk necklace, his mwali, had been blackened but remained intact against his chest.

Nobutada screamed in anguish at the sight of Majok's burns, his eyes meeting his father's across the crowd. Nobunaga stood in the rain, his expression unreadable as he watched the man who had just risked everything to save two lives.

Ostrimyo placed a hand on Nobutada's shoulder. "Quickly, we must act swiftly if we are to save him. Tears are for mourning, and we don't have time for that now."

As they carried Majok toward the medical quarters, none of them noticed the strange, sulfurous smell that lingered in the air around the destroyed building, or the way the flames had burned in colors that had no place in any natural fire.

The lightning had been the catalyst—the shokubai—but what it had ignited would change everything.

Chapter 12: The Wariat

The night had descended upon Azuchi-jo like a burial shroud, heavy with the weight of unspoken grief. A light rain began to fall, each droplet striking the wooden rooftops with the persistence of a funeral drum. The compound lay wrapped in an eerie stillness, broken only by the soft patter of water and the occasional creak of timbers settling under the dampness.

Outside the infirmary, two guards stood watch in stoic silence, their faces grave as they maintained their vigil. The flickering torches cast long, dancing shadows that seemed to writhe like spirits in the gloom, and the air itself felt thick with foreboding.

Within the pristine walls of the medical chamber, the scene was one of quiet desperation. The room, normally a place of healing, had become a shrine to suffering. Nurses moved with hushed efficiency, their white garments ghostlike in the candlelight, while Dr. Watanabe worked with the methodical precision of a man who had seen too many battles between life and death.

Majok lay motionless on the low wooden platform that served as his bed, his powerful frame reduced to a landscape of charred flesh and angry welts. The burns covered the entire left side of his body—shoulder, chest, and back—where the flames had claimed their tribute. His breathing was shallow and labored, each rise and fall of his chest a small victory against the infection that coursed through his weakened system.

Dr. Watanabe finally straightened from his examination, his weathered face bearing the expression of a man delivering news he wished he didn't have to give. He approached Ostrimyo, speaking in low, measured Japanese.

"The infection has spread faster than anticipated," the doctor said quietly. "His body is fighting, but it grows weaker by the hour.

I have done all I can with traditional medicine. Without intervention... I fear we may lose him before dawn."

Ostrimyo's scarred face remained impassive, but his hands clenched slightly at his sides. Dr. Watanabe bowed respectfully and gathered his instruments, leaving the old retainer alone with the magnitude of what he'd just heard.

Moments later, Nobutada and Sunanomi entered the chamber, their faces etched with worry and exhaustion. They had been maintaining their vigil for days, taking turns at Majok's bedside, watching for any sign of improvement that never seemed to come.

"What did the doctor say?" Nobutada asked, though the expression on Ostrimyo's face already told him much of what he needed to know.

Ostrimyo turned toward them, his voice heavy with the weight of truth. "There is little hope for his survival. The infection will overcome his body soon. He will die." He paused, then continued with quiet reverence. "He is a great warrior—he has warrior blood running through his veins. He should be offered the El Narrat—the Warrior's Death. He is worthy of that honor."

Sunanomi stepped forward, his young face fierce with determination. "No, there has to be another way. There must be something—anything—we haven't tried."

Ostrimyo was quiet for a long moment, his blind eyes seeming to look inward to some distant memory or possibility. "There is... but it's risky. The process itself could kill him. But if he survives it, he will no longer be a basic man. He will ascend to a level just beneath the angels."

Nobutada's voice was immediate and certain. "Do it!"

Ostrimyo nodded slowly, then gestured to one of the handmaids attending in the corner. She bowed and slipped silently from the room.

"What's happening?" Sunanomi asked, his eyes darting between Ostrimyo and the door through which the servant had vanished.

Ostrimyo held his words, his expression unreadable as they waited in the heavy silence. The rain continued its rhythmic assault on the roof above, and the candles flickered as if touched by unseen hands.

Nobutada stared at Majok. "It's all my fault," he whispered.

Sunanomi came to his side. "No, my lord. How could you say such a thing? No one can control the weather. That storm—"

Nobutada met Sunanmi's gaze with a slight shake of his head. "The fire. It wasn't the just the storm."

Suddenly, then the doors slid open. The figure that filled the doorframe seemed to belong to another world entirely. Tall and imposing, with strong, chiseled features that spoke of distant lands and ancient wisdom, the man was clearly not Japanese. His long beard was streaked with silver, and his eyes were a startling white with only the faintest hint of pupils visible in their depths. He wore a long ceremonial gown of Persian expression, with stark tones of beige, green, and purple. Upon his head sat a mystical hat adorned with symbols none of them recognized, and in his arms he carried a straw basket that seemed far heavier than his effortless bearing suggested.

"Welcome, Azreth," Ostrimyo said with quiet respect.

Nobutada's shock was evident in his voice. "You brought a Shaman Priest here!" The words came out more forcefully than he'd intended, but his astonishment had overtaken his composure.

"We mustn't," Sunanomi protested, taking a step backward. "This goes against—"

"This is the only way," Azreth interrupted, his voice carrying the weight of mountains and the depth of ancient rivers. "It's either this, or give your final prayers to the great African warrior."

Sunanomi looked up at the shaman with wide eyes. "How do you know he's a warrior?"

Azreth's white gaze seemed to pierce through the young man. "I felt the power emanating from this room the moment I stepped outside the door. His spirit burns brighter than his flesh, even in this darkest hour."

Sunanomi looked to Nobutada, whose face wore equal parts confusion and intrigue. The young lord stared at Majok's still form, then back at the mysterious shaman. "Do it," Nobutada commanded finally, his voice filled with desperate resolve. "Do whatever it takes."

Ostrimyo gently guided the two younger men backward, making room for Azreth as the shaman set down his basket and began to work with practiced efficiency. He moved to the corner of the room and lit a large, thick candle with an elaborate flame that seemed to burn brighter than natural fire should. Then, moving with deliberate purpose, he began extinguishing the other candles one by one until only that single, powerful light source remained.

The room transformed in the dancing shadows. What had been a place of medicine became something far more ancient and sacred.

Azreth opened his basket and withdrew items that seemed to belong to no earthly apothecary: dried herbs that caught the light like precious metals, small vials containing liquids that swirled with their own inner luminescence, and long sticks of incense that released smoke the color of storm clouds.

He began to chant in a language that predated any they had ever heard, his voice rising and falling like an ocean tide. The incense burned with tall spires of smoke that swirled to the ceiling, casting long, moving shadows across Majok's burned body. The lone candle seemed to burn brighter as the ritual progressed, as if drawing power from the shaman's words.

Azreth worked tirelessly, blowing the mystical smoke directly into Majok's face. Gradually, miraculously, the African's lungs began to rise and fall with more strength, like an angry ocean tide fighting against some unseen shore.

Then the shaman turned his attention to the burns themselves. From his basket, he withdrew a silvery, metallic solution that gleamed like liquid moonlight. As he applied it to Majok's wounds while continuing his chant, something extraordinary happened. The solution seemed to react with the rich melanin in Majok's dark skin, forming a hard, protective shielding along the burned surfaces.

Nobutada's eyes widened in amazement as he watched the transformation taking place before them. As the healing progressed, Nobutada found himself wanting more, needing the process to move faster. "Is there anything else?" he asked urgently. "I've heard of a healing root called diffillin that grows deep in the eastern woods. I have no problem venturing there if it will help him."

Azreth's response was sharp and immediate. "Silence! You know not what you speak. The woods are no place for a prince, or even a great warrior for that matter."

Sunanomi leaned forward, his curiosity overcoming his caution. "What's in the eastern woods? I've heard stories of demons. What do they want?"

Azreth's white eyes seemed to grow even paler as he continued his work on Majok's wounds. "Long ago, Chiwa was spawned into the realm of the living under evil circumstances and witchery the likes of which have never been replicated. His mother gave birth to twins, but they were being hunted by order of the VOX Legionnaire. When they finally caught up with them, tragedy struck and Chiwa was never seen again." The shaman's voice took on the quality of ancient prophecy. "But it is believed that his powers and seductive ways have earned him a realm of his own. There he waits, planning his return to destroy those of this realm. These same eastern woods possess the remnants of his followers—they pluck out warriors one by one, drawing them into Chiwa's domain. When he is strong enough, he will enact his treacherous plans of world domination."

"And what of his brother?" Sunanomi asked, his voice barely above a whisper. "Where is he now?"

But Azreth cut him off with a sharp look, his narrowed white eyes clearly indicating that some knowledge was not meant to be shared. He returned his attention to Majok, working with renewed intensity.

For what seemed like an eternity, the shaman labored over the wounded man. Sweat poured from Azreth's body as if he were being ignited by some inner fire, his chants growing more powerful, more urgent. The very air in the room seemed to thicken with mystical energy.

Finally, satisfied with his work, the ritual came to an end. Azreth turned to face the three men, his mystical hat casting strange shadows in the candlelight. "Everything Majok needs to survive is right there," he said, gesturing to the now-peaceful figure on the bed. "The herbs, the medicine, and strong spirits combined with the belief that he is worthy to pull himself from the jaws of death. The eastern woods are no place for anyone, especially the son of a daimyo. Yasuke is strong. He will recover in time."

Nobutada looked confused. "His name is Majok."

Azreth smiled mysteriously and collected his candle. As he snuffed it out, something impossible happened—all the candles that had been previously extinguished suddenly reignited simultaneously, filling the room with warm, natural light.

When they looked again, the shaman was gone.

Days Later

The great hall bore the same oppressive atmosphere that had settled over the entire compound since the fire. Rain continued to fall steadily outside, drumming against the wooden panels with relentless persistence. The assembled retainers sat in their formal positions, but there was a tension in the air that went beyond the usual political maneuvering.

Nobunaga occupied his elevated platform with an expression of barely controlled fury. To his right sat Nobutada, his face pale and drawn, while Akechi maintained his position among the other generals, wearing what could only be described as a satisfied smile.

For the first time, Ostrimyo had been invited to attend a formal council meeting, taking a position near the administrative officials. Majok's absence was felt like a missing piece in a puzzle that no longer quite fit together.

Nobunaga's voice cut through the silence like a blade. "We are here to address a matter of grave consequence that has come to my attention. My son has confessed to me in private something that affects the security of this entire domain." Nobutada's hands trembled slightly as his father continued. "The explosive Hellfire elements—extracted from volcanic sources and formulated by our head technicians—were stored incorrectly. Against my explicit instructions to place them in the outer field sheds, my son chose to store them in the slave quarters."

The revelation hit the assembled retainers like a physical blow. Akechi's smile widened slightly as he leaned forward.

"What will become of the young lord?" Akechi asked, his voice carrying a tone of false concern that fooled no one.

Nobutada stared at his father, fear evident in his eyes as he awaited his punishment. Nobunaga let the silence stretch until it became almost unbearable.

"Nobutada will be relegated to the countryside," Nobunaga announced, his voice carrying the finality of judgment. "He will utilize the remaining Hellfire chemicals to attack our enemies—the Buddhist priest sects who continue to resist our authority. He turned to face Nobutada. "You will weaponize these chemicals, creating incendiary devices to load into catapults. You will burn their villages to the ground." Nobunaga's next words came with the cold efficiency of a death sentence. "You will leave nothing standing—no women, children, men, or animals. Nothing."

Nobutada was stunned into silence, fighting to hold back tears that threatened to spill from his eyes. The emotional weight of the moment was overwhelming, and even Ostrimyo, despite his blindness, could sense the young lord's anguish. Tears began to form in the slits of the old retainer's damaged eyelids.

Even Akechi, despite his satisfaction at Nobutada's punishment, seemed alarmed by the brutality of Nobunaga's tactics. This was another crack in their relationship— historically, Akechi had always been uncomfortable with his lord's more extreme methods. He took the moment to express his discontent. "My lord," Akechi said carefully, "such complete destruction might be seen as—"

"I don't want to hear your concerns," Nobunaga cut him off sharply. "The decision is made." He turned back to his son with pitiless determination. "You will take your men and head out at sunrise. Do not return until every trace of resistance has been eliminated."

The meeting ended in heavy silence, the weight of what had just transpired settling over everyone present like a funeral shroud. As the retainers filed out, Nobutada remained seated, staring at his hands while the rain continued its relentless assault on the compound.

The wariate—the division—had been made. And in the morning, everything would change.

Chapter 13: The Dhen

Weeks Later - 1581

Time moved differently in the palace chambers where Majok lay recovering, each day stretching like a gentle tide that advanced and retreated without urgency. The room assigned to him was a testament to his elevated status—no longer the modest slave quarters, but a proper chamber within the palace walls, with sliding panels that opened to reveal carefully tended gardens and the distant mountains beyond.

Day after day, Ostrimyo and Sunanomi maintained their vigil. They would arrive each morning like clockwork, speaking in hushed tones with Dr. Watanabe and the handmaids who had been assigned to tend to Majok's wounds. The women moved with practiced efficiency, cleaning his skin with gentle precision and changing the mystical dressings that Azreth had prescribed.

"His breathing grows stronger each day," Dr. Watanabe would report, his weathered hands checking Majok's pulse and examining the burns that were healing with supernatural speed. "The infection has completely cleared. Whatever that shaman did... it defies all medical understanding."

Majok remained in a deep stupor, suspended between worlds as his body fought its way back from the edge of death. His powerful frame lay still beneath the silk coverings, but there was a sense of gathering strength, like a storm building on a distant horizon.

The most unexpected visitors came in the early mornings, when the compound was still wrapped in pre-dawn quiet. The slaves who had been relocated to temporary quarters would approach the palace steps with offerings—flowers from the rose garden, carefully arranged at the base of the stairs leading to Majok's chamber. They came silently, reverently, leaving their tokens of respect for the man who had risked everything to save one of their own.

Word of these visits reached even the highest levels of the compound. During one of his regular inspections, Nobunaga himself came to observe the recovery process. He stood in the doorway for long minutes, saying nothing, his sharp eyes taking in every detail of the care being provided. His presence commanded absolute silence from the attending staff, but there was something different in his demeanor—a quality of respect that had not been there before.

Not everyone shared this sentiment.

In the training courtyard, Akechi continued his relentless drilling of his samurai, their katas precise and deadly as they moved through their forms. When Nobunaga's procession returned from the direction of the palace chambers, Akechi's envious gaze followed them with barely concealed resentment. "Has the inu recovered from his burns?" Akechi asked one of his subordinates, his tone heavy with sarcasm as he watched Nobunaga disappear into the administrative buildings.

"His wounds are almost completely healed, General," the man replied carefully. "He will live, if that is what you're asking."

Akechi's jaw tightened. "I'm not asking out of concern. I just need him to return to his duties as soon as possible. Everyone in Azuchi-jo has a job to do. He continues to bring dishonor to this house. It would have been better if he had died."

Unknown to Akechi, Nobunaga had returned and stood within earshot, his expression darkening as he heard the general's words.

"Even in betrayal and death, honor must be preserved," Nobunaga said, stepping into view. His voice carried the weight of absolute authority. "The physician says he has a warrior's heart. Not even death can destroy that."

The words struck Akechi like a hammer, effectively silencing any further rebuttals. He bowed stiffly and returned to his training, but the fury in his eyes burned brighter than ever.

Days Later

Consciousness returned to Majok like the gradual lightening of dawn—slowly, then all at once. His eyes opened to unfamiliar surroundings, the elegant wooden beams and silk panels of the palace chamber a stark contrast to the humble quarters he remembered. Days passed like weeks as his strength gradually returned, each small movement a victory over the weakness that had claimed him.

The handmaids were gentle and efficient, helping him sit up, then stand, then take tentative steps around the room. But as he gained awareness of his surroundings, panic began to set in. His hand moved instinctively to his chest, searching for the familiar weight of his ivory elephant.

It was gone.

"Where—" Majok began in English, then switched to halting Japanese, trying to describe the precious necklace to the confused women. They looked at each other uncertainly, unable to understand what he was searching for with such desperation.

Just then, Sunanomi entered the chamber, his face lighting up with joy at seeing Majok awake and alert. "Majok-san! You have returned to us!" Sunanomi rushed to his side, his relief evident in every word.

"Sunanomi," Majok said, gripping the young man's arm. "The two girls—from the fire—did they survive?"

"Yes, both are well. You saved them both." Sunanomi's expression grew more serious. "You've been unconscious for weeks. Much has changed."

Majok's heart sank as he read the sadness in Sunanomi's face. "Nobutada... where is he?"

Sunanomi hesitated, clearly reluctant to deliver painful news. "I should tell you what I witnessed, so you understand what happened." He paused, gathering his thoughts. "It was early morning, just after the fire. I was leaving the palace when I heard voices—angry voices. I knew I shouldn't listen, but..." He looked away, clearly uncomfortable with admitting to eavesdropping. "It was Lord Nobunaga and Nobutada-sama. They were arguing. Nobutada-sama was refusing orders, saying he wouldn't comply. Lord Nobunaga told him, 'You are only a prince, you're not king.'"

Majok could picture the scene, the tension that must have filled the air. He could sense the tension of the moment, evident by Sunanomi soft words. "Go on."

"Nobutada-sama replied, 'You're not either—you're a lord.' That's when Lord Nobunaga struck him." Sunanomi's voice dropped to a mere whisper. "He dismissed him immediately."

"So he is gone?" Majok asked, though he already knew the answer.

"Yes, Majok-san," Sunanomi replied, his voice heavy with sadness.

"When will he return from this mission?"

"Time will tell," Sunanomi said carefully. Then, seeing the guilt beginning to form in Majok's eyes, he continued quickly. "The fire that night—it wasn't just the storm. Nobutada-sama had stored explosive materials in the slave quarters against his father's orders. When the lightning struck... he blamed himself for your injuries. He admitted his mistake to Lord Nobunaga and then he was sent east to destroy the remaining Buddhist faction strongholds. Using the Hellfire as the chief weapon."

Majok closed his eyes, feeling the weight of responsibility settle on his shoulders. "This is because of me. If I hadn't been burned—"

"No." The voice came from the doorway, where Ostrimyo stood with his characteristic calm presence. "Only what can happen, will. It's up to us to determine our next steps as fate continues on."

"Wing!" Majok's eyes widened as he bowed respectfully. "It is good to see you."

"And it is good to hear the drumming of your strong heart once more," Ostrimyo replied with genuine warmth. "I have brought someone to see you."

Ostrimyo clapped his hands twice, and the doors slid open to reveal a small figure—the Japanese girl Majok had rescued from the flames. She carried a small bag of sackcloth, holding it carefully as if it contained the most precious treasure in the world.

She approached with shy steps and presented the bag to Majok. With trembling hands, he opened it to reveal his ivory elephant necklace—but transformed. Where once it had been blackened and charred, it now gleamed with pristine white beauty. Every trace of ash and soot had been painstakingly removed, the elephant restored to its original glory.

Majok knelt down to receive the gift, his eyes filling with emotion as the little girl spoke to him in rapid Japanese—words he'd never heard before but whose meaning he could feel in his heart.

He looked to Sunanomi, who was beaming with joy. "She says, 'May this renewed piece of ivory bring you wealth and prosperity.'"

Majok carefully lifted the necklace over his head, feeling the familiar weight settle against his chest. Then he opened his arms and embraced the little girl, holding her close as tears of gratitude fell from his eyes. Standing, he looked down at her and spoke carefully in Japanese: "You are dhen. In my language, it means beautiful."

The girl's face lit up with delight at being understood, and she bowed deeply before backing away.

"**Come, child**," Ostrimyo said gently. "**Majok-san needs to recover his strength**." He then turned to Majok. "I will return tomorrow to take you back to the training grounds."

"Training grounds?" Majok asked, confused.

Ostrimyo's scarred face creased into a knowing smile. "Ah, Majok-san. You didn't think all this work was just for daily exercise, did you? Unfortunately, you still lack the wisdom it takes to see without eyes. Pity."

The Next Day

The morning sun streamed through the dojo's open panels as Majok practiced his forms, his movements careful but determined as he tested the limits of his recovered strength. The burns had healed completely, leaving his dark skin unmarked, as if the fire had never touched him.

He was deep in concentration when the doors slid open, and Nobunaga entered carrying two wooden practice swords. The daimyo wore a magnificent long robe that swept the floor, its rich fabric speaking of ceremony and significance.

Majok immediately stopped his practice and bowed deeply.

"I see you have returned to us," Nobunaga said, his voice carrying a weight of meaning beyond mere observation. "In my culture, when the gods send you back from the edge of death, it means there is still much for you to accomplish."

"Hopefully, I can find my way to fulfill that purpose," Majok replied respectfully.

Nobunaga began to circle him like a prowling wolf, his keen eyes taking in every detail of Majok's restored form, as if admiring the miraculous handiwork of the physicians and the handmaids, unaware of Azreth's mystical intervention. "Not a scratch on you," he observed with something approaching wonder.

Majok looked down at himself, still amazed by his complete recovery. "Yes, I am most grateful for your help and hospitality while I was recovering. The people who cared for me—they showed extraordinary kindness."

Nobunaga stopped his circling and held both wooden swords aloft, testing their weight and balance with the practiced eye of a master swordsman. Finally, seemingly satisfied with his analysis, he threw one to Majok, who caught it from the air with fluid precision.

"You have natural skill," Nobunaga acknowledged, "but you must master the sword in ways that go beyond instinct. Come—I will train you today."

What followed was unlike any training session Majok had ever experienced. Soon both men had shed their outer garments, wearing only loose white pants as they moved through increasingly complex sequences. Sweat dripped from their bodies as wooden blades clicked together in perfect rhythm, neither making contact with the other's flesh despite the speed and intensity of their movements.

"A warrior's sword is a lethal extension of his arm," Nobunaga instructed as they sparred. "Might is important, yes, but it is the steady hand that threads the needle. Finding the heart of your opponent requires precision, not just power." He demonstrated with a series of lightning-fast strikes that Majok had never witnessed before—movements that seemed to bend the very air around them. "You are strong and powerful, but you lack the finesse required to survive true battle. Too many uncontrolled swings will bring fatigue and cause your arm to betray you. Coordination and speed will be greater allies than any of your comrades."

With his final words, Nobunaga executed a perfect thrust, the tip of his wooden sword coming to rest gently against Majok's chest—a strike that would have been lethal with a real blade.

Nobunaga paused and secured his wooden sword in his belt, his breathing controlled despite the intensity of their session. For a moment, he seemed to wrestle with something internal before speaking. "My son has taken a... liking to you," he said carefully. "Are you familiar with men? In that way?"

Majok looked puzzled for a moment before understanding dawned. "No, my lord. I have only been with one woman, all my life. She bore my daughter."

Nobunaga nodded slowly. "There are whispers about Nobutada's proclivities that are... *unnatural* to some. Admittedly, he takes after his father in some ways, but where I preferred only one type, he prefers both. You are a father, so you understand how it might feel to see your children follow a path that you find... unsettling."

Majok considered his words carefully before responding. "My daughter is still very young, but yes, I do empathize with your concern. But if I may, my lord, might I offer a suggestion?"

Nobunaga nodded, his full attention focused on Majok's words.

"Unconditional love begins from the day our children enter this world," Majok said with quiet conviction. "For the majority of my life, I have had nothing. As a slave, I have endured much sorrow and pain. My only desire is to protect my daughter from that suffering—to give her a life filled with peace, love, joy, and happiness. I dream of wanting everything better for her than what I have had to endure, because that is the continuity of unconditional love. Something given for nothing in return. Accepting our children's choices maintains that kind of love."

Nobunaga stared at Majok with intense concentration, his eyes working over him like he was trying to solve some profound human puzzle. How could a man born of such turmoil possess such wisdom? He found himself wondering if he could achieve such understanding if he had endured similar hardships, and the thought humbled him.

For the first time, Nobunaga looked upon Majok not with the calculating gaze of a master evaluating a useful tool, but with genuine admiration and respect.

After a long moment of contemplation, Nobunaga finally spoke. "That is enough training for today. I will see you tomorrow."

"Tomorrow?" Majok asked, surprised.

"How else will we continue your training?" Nobunaga turned to walk away, then called out loudly, "Guards!" The doors opened immediately, and just before Nobunaga exited, he looked back at Majok one final time. "Gather your things. Tonight, you sleep in the family house."

Majok's eyes widened in astonishment as he bowed deeply. "Yes, Lord Nobunaga."

As the daimyo disappeared through the doorway, Majok touched the restored ivory elephant at his chest. The mwali had been reborn, cleansed by fire and love.

And so had he.

Chapter 14: The Obake

The morning sun cast long shadows across the dojo floor as Nobunaga and Majok continued their daily training regimen. Their practice had evolved from basic instruction to the refinement of a deadly art, each session building upon the last with methodical precision.

"We must teach you control," Nobunaga instructed as they moved through increasingly complex sequences. "Your speed and power are your greatest gifts, but they can equally be your greatest weakness. Each swing, no matter how strong or weak, must be governed by absolute control."

Their wooden swords clicked together in rapid succession, neither man giving ground as they flowed through their forms.

"You cannot overexert yourself," Nobunaga continued, his breathing steady despite the intensity of their sparring. "A battle can rage for days and nights. Too much effort lessens the quality of the work. In a fight, loss of control can be fatal." He executed a perfect sequence of strikes that forced Majok to retreat several steps. "Be like wind—flow where and how you desire. Never dance to the tune of your enemy."

As their session concluded, Majok bowed respectfully and began to gather his equipment. The sound of approaching footsteps announced Akechi's arrival, his timing as perfectly calculated as everything else about the man.

Nobunaga was cleaning his hands with a fresh, warm towel provided by one of his servant girls when Akechi spoke, his voice tight with barely controlled frustration.

"Why do you train this inu?" Akechi demanded. "He is not a warrior and he will never be samurai. You further disgrace this house by—"

"Silence, General." Nobunaga's voice cut through the air like a blade. "And I am forbidding you to ever speak to me again out of turn with your suggestions or comments unless they are solicited. It will be punishable by death. Understood?"

Akechi's jaw clenched, but he bowed stiffly. "Understood, daimyo."

Nobunaga turned hi back to Akechi, arms folded behind his back. "Any reports from Nobutada on his progress?"

"No, daimyo."

"Then you know what your duties are for today," Nobunaga said as he slightly turned his head in Akechi's direction. "You are dismissed."

Akechi departed with obvious reluctance, his frustration radiating from every step.

The Next Morning

Another dawn found Nobunaga and Majok once again engaged in their training, but this session carried a different focus—one of deadly precision rather than raw power.

"Today, I will teach you my personal kata," Nobunaga announced, as he stood tall and then slumped into a defensive posture, holding his sword protectively across his body. "Wait, parry, and strike. Wait, parry, and strike," he repeated as his body moved swiftly, reflecting only two-thirds of the commands from his mouth. "Your enemies will assume that your size dictates your skill. They will expect you to rely on unbridled aggression and will anticipate violent and wild attacks from you. But what if you show them something altogether different—something foreign to their thought processes?"

Majok considered this strategy. "So am I to suppress all of my attacks? If my power is my strength, when do I use it?"

"There is a time and purpose for everything," Nobunaga replied. "Your power—keep it, train it. Against the unskilled, yes, use it without restraint. But for those who are more refined, you must counter-attack and confuse them."

Mojak raised an eyebrow at him his mind racing to understand what his newly minted instructor was trying to convey. Nobunaga sensed that he was struggling with the concept and decided to provide a complete demonstration. So, Nobunaga performed the kata again, this time, fully executing the moves. He was both fluid and deceptive. What appeared to be a defensive stance suddenly exploded into a devastating offensive combination, culminating in a powerful thrust accompanied by a sharp *kiai* that echoed through the dojo. He held the final position for several seconds before relaxing. "Short, quick, effective, and intentional thrusts," he explained. "The power flows from your core, through your shoulder, down through the elbow, and finally out of your wrist. The sword—the deadly extension of a samurai's arm."

Majok nodded, absorbing the instruction. "How do you know what they will expect?"

For the first time, Nobunaga's stern expression softened into something approaching a smile. "Because I would expect the same. Now, you try."

Majok set himself in the proper stance, centering his breathing as Ostrimyo had taught him months ago. He began the sequence slowly, building momentum until the final explosive thrust erupted with surprising power and precision. To both his and Nobunaga's amazement, he held the pose perfectly, breaking form only when he heard the sound of enthusiastic clapping.

"Excellent," Nobunaga said with genuine approval. "You learn quickly."

The Following Day

The war council gathered in the great hall, military advisors arranged in careful order of rank and experience. Intelligence reports had finally arrived regarding Nobutada's campaigns in the eastern territories, and the news was mixed.

"Nobutada-sama has been successful in crushing resistance in the Mikawa and Totomi regions," General Sassa reported, consulting his scrolls. "The Buddhist strongholds at Kanegasaki and Odawara have been reduced to ash, as ordered. However, we have encountered an unexpected development."

Nobunaga's expression sharpened. "Continue."

"In his absence, certain ninja sects affiliated with the opposing Buddhist armies have rallied. These shinobi—the shadow warriors who serve the militant Buddhist leagues—have proven more resilient than anticipated." The general's voice carried a note of concern. "The Sōhei warrior monks we thought were destroyed have regrouped under new leadership in the mountain regions."

Another advisor stepped forward. "My lord, a coalition of these forces has taken control of a strategic supply depot near the Tenryu River. They've trapped a small battalion of our forces and are using the position as both a rallying point and a base for launching raids against our supply lines. The village depends on that depot for food and provisions."

"What of their leadership?" Nobunaga asked.

"They are commanded by someone known only as the Obake—'the shape-shifter,'" the first general replied. "Intelligence suggests he was once a samurai who turned to the ninja arts after his clan was destroyed. Our scouts report he possesses both traditional samurai training and the unconventional warfare techniques of the shinobi."

The assembled advisors exchanged concerned glances before one spoke up. "My lord, our forces are stretched thin with the eastern campaigns. Perhaps we should ignore this threat until we can consolidate our position."

Nobunaga's response was immediate and decisive. "Absolutely not. They are a cancer to the kingdom. And if a cancer is allowed to fester without treatment, it can grow and infect many other healthy cells. Before long, the entire body is contaminated and it's too late to destroy it. No, we must eliminate this threat completely while it is still weak and before they can establish a permanent foothold in the region." He looked across the room to where Majok stood at attention near the back wall. "Do you have any suggestions?"

"Me, Lord Nobunaga?" Majok asked, clearly surprised to be consulted.

"You worked under many military leaders during your time as a slave, didn't you? Surely you witnessed various military strategies," Nobunaga replied.

"I did, Lord Nobunaga," Majok said carefully.

Nobunaga pressed further. "Well, what did you observe?"

Before Majok could respond, Akechi's voice cut through the room as others mumbled amongst themselves. "What? From this fool?"

Nobunaga raised his hand sharply. The room grew silent. "You were saying, Majok?"

Majok gathered his thoughts before responding. "Well, I may not have witnessed such a dilemma in a formal war, but I do recall something from my time in the Middle East with the Portuguese missionaries. We were involved in a small skirmish in Morocco. A ruling warlord had illegally invaded a town and was fortified in a farmhouse. No one could penetrate their defenses because it was heavily protected by mercenaries with firearms." He paused, organizing his memories. "But the back of the farm was adjacent to dense forest. There was a slight chance to overcome them at precisely the right time, with the proper diversion. We chose to send the majority of our men to attack from the rear, but only after we set the front farmyard ablaze. As the animals panicked and reacted to the flames, the defenders abandoned their posts to control the chaos. That's when we launched our assault, each man armed with his preferred weapon—some with muskets, others with clubs and swords. I carried my spear."

Majok's eyes seemed to focus on something beyond the present moment. "It was the first time I'd experienced battle of such magnitude, and also the first time I felt my spear pierce a man's chest." He paused, clearly reliving the memory. "The victory was swift and decisive. We could employ similar tactics here—coordinate with our trapped forces to mount pressure from the front while we execute a silent assault from behind. Just a few skilled men would be sufficient."

"We?" Akechi interjected with obvious disdain. "This inu thinks he's going to—what a joke. My bow is greater than his entire body. I can clear out that compound myself, without his aid. I'm not going anywhere with him."

Nobunaga stood slowly. "You are correct, Akechi." Akechi smirked triumphantly at Majok before Nobunaga continued. "Your bow is as legendary as your reputation as a skilled leader. But you will not go. Majok will proceed without you."

"What?" Akechi's composure cracked completely.

"Recall our last conversation, General," Nobunaga reminded him with deadly calm.

Akechi clenched his jaw but held his tongue.

Nobunaga turned to General Sassa. "Notify our forces in the region of the plan. Take ten samurai with you. You will lead this assault, and Majok will serve as your second-in-command." He then addressed Majok directly. "You have experience with cleaning samurai armor, haven't you?"

"Yes, Lord Nobunaga," Majok replied.

Nobunaga nodded. "Good. Then you understand the components well enough to help the others prepare. For this mission, you will wear only a breastplate, greaves, and boots. I want you faster than any samurai out there. You will surprise and eliminate anyone in your path. Understood?"

Majok bowed deeply. "Yes, Lord Nobunaga."

The Next Morning

The expedition departed at dawn, a small but elite force moving swiftly through the mountainous terrain toward the contested region. The journey took them through ancient forests where the shinobi were known to hide, and past abandoned Buddhist temples that bore the scars of recent conflicts.

General Sassa proved to be an efficient commander, and by midday they had reached the rendezvous point where scouts provided final intelligence on the enemy positions.

"The Obake has positioned his forces cleverly," the lead scout reported. "The depot sits in a natural valley with only two approaches—the main road from the south, and a narrow mountain path from the north. Our trapped forces hold defensive positions along the southern approach, but they're running low on supplies."

Majok studied the rough map scratched in the dirt. "How many defenders?"

"Perhaps thirty ninja and warrior monks, plus the Obake himself. They've been using hit-and-run tactics, striking our supply lines and disappearing back into the mountains."

General Sassa nodded grimly. "We'll implement the strategy as discussed. Half our force will create a diversion at the southern entrance while the rest of us approach from the north. Majok, you'll spearhead the assault once we're in position. Any questions?"

"One. How will I know what the Obake looks like? How many defenders?" Majok asked.

"He is big, and strong—with a similar build to you, with the exception of a larger stomach. Obake means ghost in our language. He has wild, long grey hair and fittingly wears kumadori face paint of red and black. It symbolizes both anger and darkness. When you see him, you'll know," General Sassa replied.

The Assault

As evening approached, the plan unfolded with precise timing. The diversionary force engaged the enemy from the south, drawing the majority of defenders away from the depot itself. Meanwhile, Majok led the northern assault team through treacherous mountain paths, moving like shadows through the gathering darkness.

The initial phase went flawlessly. Majok's combination of size, speed, and unconventional techniques caught the enemy completely off guard. His movements flowed between the African martial arts Ostrimyo had helped him refine and the precise sword work Nobunaga had drilled into him.

One by one, the outer sentries fell to his blade, their deaths silent and swift. The other samurai followed his lead, systematically clearing the perimeter until they reached the main compound.

That's when the Obake appeared.

Large and ominous, the enemy commander seemed to materialize from the shadows themselves, his dark clothing and face paint making him nearly invisible in the twilight. He was larger than Majok had expected, but his movements carried the fluid grace of a smaller, master warrior.

"Fan out and finish off the others," Majok commanded. The samurai followed his orders and quickly emptied the area, leaving him all along with the Obake.

"So," the Obake said in accented Japanese, "the foreign giant comes to play samurai."

Obake and Majok rushed to the center of the open space. Their blades met with a ringing crash that echoed across the valley as sparks lit the darkness.

What followed was unlike any combat Majok had ever experienced. The Obake fought with a style that seamlessly blended traditional samurai sword work with the deceptive, unpredictable techniques of the ninja. He would attack conventionally, then suddenly drop low for a leg sweep, or leap impossibly high to strike from above.

Majok found himself forced to draw upon every skill he had learned—Ostrimyo's lessons about flowing like grass in the wind, Nobunaga's teachings about control and precision, even the raw survival instincts from his days as a captured warrior in Africa.

The fight raged across the compound, neither man able to gain a decisive advantage. The Obake was faster and more experienced, but Majok's reach and power kept him competitive. Gradually, however, the extended combat began to take its toll.

Majok's breathing grew labored, his movements slightly less crisp. The Obake sensed this weakness and pressed his advantage, launching a series of increasingly aggressive attacks that Majok struggled to repel.

Just when exhaustion threatened to overwhelm him, Nobunaga's voice echoed in Majok's memory: "*Be like wind—flow where and how you desire. Never dance to the tune of your enemy.*"

Majok suddenly stopped trying to match the Obake's frantic pace. Instead, he centered himself, waiting for the perfect moment. When the enemy commander committed to what he thought would be a finishing thrust, Majok executed Nobunaga's personal kata with flawless precision.

Wait. Parry. Strike.

The sequence unfolded in perfect slow motion. Majok sidestepped the attack, deflected the blade with minimal effort, and drove his sword forward in one fluid motion. The point found its mark, piercing the Obake's heart with surgical accuracy.

The enemy commander's eyes widened in surprise and what might have been respect before he collapsed to his knees, his hands desperately clinching the blade.

As news of their leader's death spread, the remaining defenders scattered into the mountains, just as Nobunaga had predicted. The depot was secured, the trapped forces freed, and the immediate threat neutralized.

The men around him celebrated, their eyes all centered on Majok as he stood over his fallen opponent. It was then that Majok felt something fundamental shift within him. He was no longer just a slave who had learned to fight, or even a skilled warrior serving a master.

He had become something new entirely.

Something the world would soon know.

Chapter 15: The Ya

The great hall had been transformed for celebration. Red and gold banners hung from the wooden beams, their silk surfaces catching the warm glow of countless paper lanterns. The victory over the Obake had rippled through the compound like wildfire, lifting spirits that had been dampened by weeks of uncertainty and conflict.

Tables arranged in precise rows displayed an abundance of traditional delicacies: steaming bowls of miso soup with delicate tofu cubes floating like clouds, grilled fish seasoned with sweet soy glaze, perfectly formed onigiri rice balls wrapped in crisp nori, and an array of pickled vegetables that added bright splashes of color to the feast. Sake flowed freely from ceramic vessels, while the air filled with the mingled aromas of jasmine tea and incense.

At the head table, Majok sat as the guest of honor, still somewhat uncomfortable with the attention but gracious in accepting the accolades of his fellow warriors. The formal seating arrangement had been adjusted at his specific request—the slaves who had once viewed him with suspicion now sat among the celebration, their faces reflecting a mixture of pride and wonder at their elevated status for the evening—a condition Majok formally requested of Nobunaga.

The traditional elements of the feast unfolded with ceremonial precision. Each course was presented with reverent attention to aesthetic beauty—the arrangement of food on lacquered plates, the careful folding of silk napkins, the ritualistic pouring of sake accompanied by respectful bows. Conversations flowed in the melodic cadences of Japanese, punctuated by occasional bursts of laughter as warriors shared embellished versions of the recent victory.

As the evening progressed and the formal presentations concluded, Ostrimyo approached Majok's position. The old retainer moved unsteadily as he walked—somewhat uncharacteristically different from his usual deliberate pace—as his scarred face bore an expression of deep satisfaction. Majok noticed and offered a supportive hand to him. "Are you okay Wing?"

"Yes, I am quite fine," Ostrimyo said as he straightened. "You have brought great honor to yourself and to this house." His voice carried the weight of genuine pride. "You stand on the cusp of a great future as a noble warrior."

Majok shook his head gently. "Wing, I appreciate your words, but I cannot accept such titles. I have only one focus—returning to my family. Though I will admit," he paused, a slight smile crossing his features, "I did appreciate the rush of battle. There was something... awakening about it."

Ostrimyo's weathered hands clasped together as he nodded knowingly. "Savor that feeling, Majok-san. There is more to come, I believe. But I'm afraid to admit that the sake has taken hold of my spirit."

"I suspected as much," Majok said with a grin.

Ostrimyo snickered. "Well, this old frame also requires rest now." He reached out and placed a gentle hand on Majok's arm, squeezing with paternal affection. "I bid you farewell for this evening."

Majok grasped Ostrimyo's hand firmly, the handshake lingering as both men seemed to sense the significance of the moment. "Please, let me accompany you home."

"Nonsense," Ostrimyo objected. "You will do no such thing. Am I too old to take myself home on this beautiful night? It's not the first time I've navigated these palace walls under influence of more than just my mind."

"Fine. Rest well, Wing. And thank you again for everything you've taught me."

As Ostrimyo made his way slowly from the hall, Nobunaga appeared at Majok's side. "Would you join me on the palace balcony? I'd like to speak with you privately."

From across the hall, Akechi's eyes followed their movement with calculating intensity. As the two men disappeared through the doorway, he quietly faded into the shadows, his expression unreadable.

The two men silently climbed a few flights of stairs before arriving at the desired placed. The balcony overlooked the compound's main courtyard, where the celebration continued below. Paper lanterns strung between buildings cast dancing shadows, and the distant sound of laughter drifted upward on the evening breeze.

"I want to personally thank you for your heroism," Nobunaga began, his formal tone softening slightly. "Your success carved deep into enemy morale and sent a clear message to the surrounding factions that the Oda clan can and will protect this region at all costs, even with diminished forces."

"It was my pleasure, Lord Nobunaga."

"I know your freedom is very important to you, and I think it's time to—"

A piercing female shriek shattered the peaceful evening air, echoing across the compound with such anguish that both men froze instantly. The sound was followed by another voice—male, younger, crying out in obvious distress.

Without hesitation, Majok vaulted over the balcony railing and dropped to the courtyard below, his feet hitting the ground running as he sprinted toward the source of the screams. Behind him, Nobunaga's heavier footsteps followed as quickly as dignity would allow.

The scene that greeted them was one of devastating finality. In a quiet corner of the compound, near the garden where Ostrimyo often walked in meditation, a small crowd had gathered around a crumpled figure. Sunanomi knelt beside the body, his young face streaked with tears as he looked up helplessly at the approaching figures.

Majok pushed through the gathered servants and guards, dropping to his knees beside Ostrimyo's still form. The old retainer lay on his side, his weathered face peaceful despite the violence of his death. Protruding from his back, having pierced completely through his heart, was a single arrow—its fletching bearing distinctive markings that Majok didn't recognize but somehow felt he should.

"Get everyone back," Majok commanded, his voice thick with emotion as he gathered Ostrimyo's body into his arms. The old man's frame felt impossibly light, as if death had already begun to hollow him out. "Wing... Wing, can you hear me?"

But even as he spoke, Majok knew it was too late. Ostrimyo's skin had already taken on the waxy pallor of death, and his eyes—those eyes that had seen so much despite their blindness—stared sightlessly at the darkening sky.

"Get Dr. Watanabe," Majok shouted to Sunanomi, desperation overriding logic. "Hurry!"

"I fear it is too late, Majok-san," Sunanomi replied gently, his own voice breaking with grief.

"No! There's still time," Majok insisted, though his hands trembled as he felt the coldness of Ostrimyo's skin. The arrow remained embedded in the old man's chest, and something told Majok that removing it would only make things worse—if such a thing were even possible.

At that moment, Akechi emerged from the shadows at the edge of the courtyard. "A sect of ninjas was spotted leaving the area, heading south, shortly after the screams began," he announced to the gathered crowd. His eyes found Majok with laser precision. "Must have been in retaliation for the recent attack. I sent some men to follow their trail."

Nobunaga finally reached the scene, taking in the tragic tableau with the grim expression of a man who had witnessed too much death in his lifetime. He placed a heavy hand on Majok's shoulder.

"Leave me with him," Nobunaga commanded quietly.

At once, samurai and servants began ushering the crowd away from the area, giving their lord private moments with his most trusted retainer. Majok rose slowly, his clothes stained with blood that wasn't his own, his heart heavy with a grief that felt like a physical weight in his chest.

As he walked away from the scene, the full magnitude of the loss began to settle over him. Every moment when he seemed to find peace, when acceptance and freedom appeared within reach, something terrible happened to shatter that hope. The pattern was becoming clear, and with that clarity came a burning rage that threatened to consume him.

Unable to contain the fury building within him, Majok lashed out at one of the thick straw support posts of a nearby storage hut. His fist connected with devastating force, causing the post to snap and part of the structure to sag dangerously. The physical pain in his knuckles was nothing compared to the anguish in his heart.

Later That Night

The compound had settled into an uneasy quiet, the celebration's joy replaced by the somber reality of loss. Majok stood alone on the palace balcony, his eyes fixed on the southern forest where Akechi claimed the assassins had fled. The darkness seemed to mock him, hiding secrets that might never be revealed.

The soft sound of approaching footsteps cut through the calming breeze of the night, announcing Nobunaga's arrival. The daimyo moved to stand beside Majok, both men gazing out at the same ominous landscape.

"There have been no signs of the ninjas in the southern forest thus far, but my men will find them," Nobunaga said, his voice carrying the weight of a promise.

"If there is someone to find," Majok replied quietly.

Nobunaga turned to study his profile. "If? What do you mean?"

Majok chose his words carefully. "What if the attacker is still within the compound? I know I'm just beginning to understand these conflicts, but from what I've observed about ninja tactics, this method of attack seems... unusual. Your safety could be compromised, daimyo."

"I agree we must take all necessary precautions to secure the area. And I can protect myself when needed. For now, I am more concerned with you." Nobunaga paused, gathering his thoughts. "You gave me some advice earlier about my son. Do you recall?"

"Yes."

"Grant me a moment to return the favor."

"Certainly, Lord Nobunaga."

"I know you are both angry and hurt by this loss. But instead of letting those emotions overwhelm and consume you, consider channeling that anger toward a new path. Help me eliminate these remaining threats, and I will grant you your freedom. You have my word."

Majok nodded slowly. "I will."

Nobunaga studied him for a long moment before continuing. "Tell me, what does your name mean in your native tongue?"

"It means 'black and white bull'—a very powerful symbol in my culture."

"As it shall be in Japanese culture as well." Nobunaga's voice took on the formal cadence of ceremony. "From now on, you will be known as Yasuke, my arrow. Arrows hold deep significance in samurai tradition—archery is one of our martial arts, arrows are used in ceremonies, and they serve as symbols of direction and purpose."

Majok—now Yasuke—looked down at his hands, still stained with Ostrimyo's blood. "But I am no samurai, Lord Nobunaga."

"From now on," Nobunaga declared with quiet authority, "you are."

The transformation was complete. Standing on that balcony under the star-filled sky, with the memory of Ostrimyo's gentle guidance still fresh in his heart and the promise of justice burning in his soul, Yasuke was born.

The ya— the arrow had found its target. Now it would seek its mark.

Chapter 16: The Saikuo

The ceremonial grounds had been prepared with the reverent precision that befitted a man of Ostrimyo's stature. White silk banners bearing the Oda mon fluttered in the morning breeze, while incense burners released fragrant clouds that seemed to carry prayers skyward. The assembled mourners—samurai, servants, and slaves alike—formed careful ranks around the raised platform where Ostrimyo's body lay in state.

Yasuke stood at the foot of the funeral pyre, clutching the Wing's wooden walking stick in his trembling hands. The familiar grooves worn smooth by years of use felt like the only real thing in a world that had suddenly become uncertain and dangerous. Beside the body lay other personal effects that would accompany Ostrimyo on his final journey: his practice sword, a small scroll containing his favorite poem, and a piece of silk fabric from his formal robes.

Dr. Watanabe stepped forward to perform the traditional Buddhist rites, his voice carrying the ancient chants that would guide the departed soul to its next existence. The ceremony proceeded with the measured cadence of centuries-old tradition—prayers offered, incense burned, and final respects paid by those whose lives had been touched by the old retainer's wisdom.

As the moment for ignition arrived, Yasuke watched the flames catch and spread across the carefully arranged wood. The fire grew quickly, consuming the physical form of the man who had been a father, teacher, and guide all in one. Through the dancing flames and rising smoke, Yasuke's eyes wandered across the assembled mourners, noting the genuine grief on most faces.

Then he saw Akechi.

Standing on the opposite side of the pyre, the general's expression was not one of mourning but of barely concealed satisfaction. There was something in his eyes—a smugness, a self-satisfied gleam that cut through Yasuke like a blade. As their gazes met through the funeral flames, Akechi's lips curved into the faintest suggestion of a smile.

In that instant, everything clicked into place with horrifying clarity.

The legendary bow. The convenient timing of the "ninja" sighting heading south. The too-perfect explanation delivered with practiced ease. Akechi's absence from the celebration just before Ostrimyo's death. His immediate appearance afterward with a ready-made story.

Yasuke's grip on the walking stick tightened until his knuckles went white, the wood creaking under the pressure. Rage built in his chest like molten metal, threatening to explode outward in a display that would honor no one, least of all Ostrimyo's memory. Through sheer force of will, he maintained his composure, but the fire in his eyes promised a reckoning that would come.

The Next Day

The war council convened in the great hall with an air of celebration that felt almost inappropriate so soon after the funeral. Maps covered the long table, marked with the territories that had fallen under Oda control, while detailed reports lay stacked beside inkwells and brushes.

Nobunaga sat at the head of the table, his presence commanding absolute attention from the assembled generals and advisors. To his right, a new chair had been placed—one meant for

Yasuke, though he remained standing at attention near the wall, still processing his elevated status.

General Sassa rose to address the assembly, his voice carrying the enthusiasm of a man delivering exceptional news. "Great and powerful daimyo, your achievements are unmatched among all lords. You pioneered the use of arquebus in large formations, organizing three-thousand-man units that employ rotating firing lines. No enemy can stand against such coordinated firepower."

Another general, Niwa Nagahide, stepped forward eagerly. "And we must not forget your first major victory at the Battle of Okehazama in 1560, where you defeated Imagawa Yoshimoto himself! You outmaneuvered an army of twenty-five thousand with just three thousand men using surprise tactics that have become legend."

"Your strategic alliance with Tokugawa Ieyasu in 1562 transformed the political landscape," added a third advisor. "Without that partnership, the Oda clan could never have achieved such dominance. Soon, my lord, you will surely be named Shogun."

The recounting continued with systematic precision as another advisor chimed in. "You captured Mino Province by 1567, establishing an unshakeable power base. Your armies have grown to command approximately one hundred thousand troops at peak strength, with your core elite force of thirty thousand directly loyal to you personally."

As the praise continued, Yasuke found himself genuinely impressed by the scope of Nobunaga's achievements. These weren't mere boasts but documented facts that painted a picture of military genius operating on a scale he had never imagined.

But something in Nobunaga's expression suggested the accolades brought him little joy. The daimyo's face had grown thoughtful, almost melancholy, as memories seemed to surface unbidden.

"I understand the fate of leaders in wartime," Nobunaga said quietly, his voice cutting through the celebration. "I have led hundreds of campaigns and built what many consider an invincible army. I have developed more mobile forces than my predecessors and studied extensively the journals and histories of great military minds." He paused, his gaze growing distant. "Yet it saddens me to read how so many great kingdoms have fallen—not by the hands of their enemies, but by those closest to them. This knowledge weighs heavily when one's own son is separated by necessity of war."

The mention of betrayal seemed to trigger a deeper memory. Nobunaga's eyes focused on something beyond the present moment as he continued.

"It reminds me of my own experience with treachery within the family..."

Fifteen Years Earlier

The battlefield stretched across the valley like a patchwork of death and determination. The enemy had taken position on higher ground, their banners snapping in the autumn wind. Among them, Nobunaga's spies had identified a figure that made his blood run cold—his uncle, Oda Nobumitsu, standing alongside the enemy commanders.

"My lord," a younger Akechi had said, raising his bow with an arrow nocked, "allow me to cut down this treacherous dog for you. One shot is all I need."

But Nobunaga had waved him off, dismounting his horse with deliberate ceremony. His samurai armor gleamed in the afternoon sun as he methodically removed his sword and placed it in his horse's saddle. The upper plates of armor followed, handed to an armor bearer who stood ready with his formal robe.

Donning the rich silk garment, Nobunaga had walked across the battlefield toward his uncle, each step measured and purposeful. The fighting around them seemed to pause as both armies recognized the significance of the confrontation.

"After all these years of hiding in shadows, waging this silent war of envy against me, you finally show your face," Nobunaga had called out when he was within speaking distance. "What is it you require of me, Uncle?"

The older man had bowed with exaggerated ceremony, his voice dripping with false humility. "I want to offer my unwavering loyalty to you, nephew."

"As I thought—you still lack the honor it takes to face a real leader." Nobunaga had turned to walk away, deliberately offering his back as the ultimate insult.

That's when his uncle had screamed, "Don't you disrespect me by showing your back!" The hidden knife had appeared from within his robes as he lunged forward.

But Nobunaga had been prepared. The sword concealed in his leg greaves slid free in one fluid motion as he spun, the blade completing a perfect arc that separated his uncle's head from his shoulders in a single cut.

"From that day forward," Nobunaga concluded, returning to the present, "it has been known as the Day of Hainin—the day when family trust was forever broken."

The war room fell silent as the implications of the story settled over the assembled generals. Akechi's face remained carefully neutral, but Yasuke caught the subtle tightening around his eyes, the almost imperceptible shift in his posture that suggested the tale had struck closer to home than comfortable.

General Niwa cleared his throat diplomatically. "With such wisdom guiding us, my lord, our position grows stronger daily. Intelligence reports suggest we may soon recruit additional forces from allied daimyo. Our numbers could swell significantly beyond current strength."

Nobunaga nodded, his strategic mind already moving past old grievances to future campaigns. "With our remaining troops, we will mobilize ashigaru formations using combined-arms tactics. I intend to invest heavily in our newly formed navy to control the Inland Sea and Lake Biwa—control of these waterways will be essential for our next phase." He stood, his presence filling the room with renewed purpose. "We will march against the Takeda clan, but first, I must honor my word to our allies. We will subjugate the Iga province ninja clans once and for all."

Applause rang out from the hands of the men around the table, except for Akechi who was too preoccupied with the daimyo—his eyes carefully following Nobunaga's gaze as it found Yasuke across the room.

"This brings me to an important appointment," Nobunaga said. "Yasuke will serve as my personal bodyguard during these campaigns."

The announcement hit the room like a physical force. Several generals shifted uncomfortably, while others nodded with grudging acceptance. But it was Akechi's reaction that caught Yasuke's attention—the general's jaw clenched so tightly that the muscles stood out like cords, and his hands curled into fists at his sides.

"Come with me, Yasuke," Nobunaga commanded as he stood. "I have something for you."

The Armory

Nobunaga 's personal armory occupied a chamber deep within the palace, its walls lined with weapons that represented decades of conquest and achievement. Each piece had been carefully maintained and displayed, creating a museum of warfare that spoke to the daimyo's appreciation for the tools of his trade.

"These are not merely weapons," Nobunaga explained as they entered the hallowed space. "They are the instruments through which history is written."

He approached a display where three particular swords rested on silk-covered stands, each one radiating an aura of legend and power.

"This is Samonji," he said, indicating the first blade. "Also known as Yoshimoto Samonji, it was taken as a trophy after my victory at the Battle of Okehazama. Every time I look upon it, I remember the moment when a small force of determined warriors overcame impossible odds through superior strategy."

Moving to the second sword, his voice took on an almost reverent tone. "Behold Heshikiri Hasebe, known for its ability to cut through anything with minimal pressure. This has been my personal blade in every major campaign. Its edge has never failed me, and its balance is without equal."

Finally, he gestured to the third weapon, smaller than the others but no less impressive. Yasuke followed Nobunaga's hands. Slowly the last weapon zoomed into focus. The gleam from the tightly, leather wrapped hilt caught the glimmer from the torches in the room and seemed to speak to Yasuke before Nobunaga could utter a word. Immediately, it beckoned for his attention. "And this brings me to Kotegiri Masamune. This sword earned its name for its ability to cut through samurai arm guards as if they were paper. I had it shortened to its current length, making it perfect for close-quarter combat—ideal for someone who is strong and powerful, yet skillful in his movements as a true samurai." Yasuke could barely pull his eyes from the blade which glowed in a green and black aura that reminded him of his motherland.

"Very impressive indeed. What samurai commands such an honor?" Yasuke asked.

Nobunaga turned from the display to face Yasuke directly, his expression solemn with ceremony. "Kotegiri is now yours, Yasuke-san."

For a moment, Yasuke could only stare at the offered blade, overwhelmed by the magnitude of the honor being bestowed upon him. Nobunaga retrieved the blade from the display and extended it to Yasuke. When Yasuke finally found his voice, it came out as barely a whisper. "Arigato gozaimasu, Nobunaga-sama," he managed in careful Japanese, accepting the sword with hands that trembled slightly.

The weight of the blade felt perfect in his grip, as if it had been waiting for him specifically. He moved through a few practice cuts, executing Nobunaga's personal kata with fluid precision before returning to a position of respectful attention.

"This honor is not lost on me, Lord Nobunaga," Yasuke said, his voice thick with emotion. "I will use it well and make you proud."

Nobunaga's stern expression softened into something approaching paternal pride. "Oh, I have a feeling you will do much better than that, Yasuke-san." He paused, his next words carrying the weight of prophecy and challenge combined. "Make Ostrimyo prouder."

Standing in that armory, holding a blade that had been wielded by legends, Yasuke felt the final pieces of his transformation lock into place. He was no longer the broken slave who had arrived at Azuchi-jo, nor even the skilled warrior who had proven himself in battle.

He was Yasuke, samurai of the Oda clan, keeper of Ostrimyo's memory, and the arrow that would soon strike into the hearts of Nobunaga's enemies.

The saikuo—the final tempering—was complete.

Chapter 17: The Senso

Late 1581

The war room at Azuchi-jo had been transformed into a strategic nerve center, its walls lined with detailed maps of Iga Province marked with enemy positions, supply routes, and potential attack corridors. The assembled generals sat in careful formation around the long table, their faces bearing the grim satisfaction of men about to embark on a campaign they knew they would win.

General Sassa stood beside the largest map, his pointer indicating key positions as he delivered his assessment. "Intelligence reports confirm approximately ten thousand ninja and local defenders scattered throughout the mountain strongholds of Iga Province. They've had months to prepare defensive positions, and they are dug in deeper in the fortified hills and forests posing a substantial threat to our advances. But their numbers are insufficient against a coordinated assault, giving us a potent advantage."

General Niwa nodded in agreement. He stood and joined General Sassa. "Our projections suggest a campaign duration of two to three months at maximum, assuming standard siege tactics and seasonal weather considerations. As General Sassa said, the mountain terrain will present challenges, but nothing insurmountable for properly trained warriors and coordinated forces."

Nobunaga sat at the head of the table, his presence commanding absolute attention. To his right, Yasuke occupied a chair that had become his customary position during war councils—a visible symbol of his elevated status that never failed to draw venomous glances from Akechi, who sat to Nobunaga's left.

"Your assessment of their capabilities?" Nobunaga asked, his gaze settling on Yasuke.

"From what I understand of ninja tactics, my lord, they excel at unconventional warfare—hit-and-run attacks, sabotage, and guerrilla tactics in terrain they know intimately. They are exceptionally fast and skilled, making them formidable opponents in direct confrontation. Our troops will need clear direction to guarantee success."

Akechi's voice cut through the discussion like a blade. "They are no match for true samurai. Our men are adept and powerful warriors, lacking the normal limitations of most men. If you were an actual samurai, you would understand this fundamental truth."

The insult hung in the air like incense smoke, but Yasuke maintained his composure as he turned toward Nobunaga. "Lord Nobunaga, I meant no disrespect to our capabilities or the skill set our men. Yet I believe it is wiser to respect our enemy rather than underestimate them. We must preserve as many warriors as possible for ongoing campaigns. If General Sassa is correct about this war requiring two to three months, we need to be strategic to maintain our fighting strength and sustain resources."

"What would you suggest?" Nobunaga asked.

Yasuke's gaze slowly swept the room before landing on Nobunaga. "I suggest we confound them to maintain the element of surprise and eliminate as many as possible through superior positioning. Outnumber them and maintain the higher ground where appropriate."

Nobunaga leaned back in his chair, his calculating mind working through the implications. "Elaborate."

"Yes. Multiple attack vectors, my lord. Instead of a single massive assault, we deploy forces from different directions simultaneously. The ninja expect unconventional tactics—we give them conventional strategy executed unconventionally," Yasuke replied.

"Wisdom," Nobunaga declared with evident satisfaction. "In Nobutada's absence, we will send Nobukatsu to lead the northern assault, supported by seasoned generals. Additional forces will approach from south and east, creating a coordinated encirclement."

Akechi leaned forward, his tone carrying carefully measured concern. "My lord, Nobukatsu lacks extensive combat experience. Perhaps this campaign is premature for such responsibility."

"Perhaps," Nobunaga acknowledged. "But with forty to fifty thousand troops at our disposal, he will have sufficient support. Besides, he needs to prove himself if he is to participate in our assault on the Takeda clan in the months ahead. Why not begin here?"

Akechi bowed stiffly. "As you wish, Lord Nobunaga-sama."

"Then it is settled. Begin preparations to fortify our armor and mobilize the men. We need precise attack formations for our infantry, continually evolving from previous cavalry battles. I want to keep the enemy on their heels. We will continue to exert our dominance against these other, less powerful daimyo. Everything needs to run smoothly. As Yasuke-san has said, we cannot afford any loses beyond what is predicted, if we are to be successful in the coming months against Takeda clan, " Nobunaga said.

"And what about our armaments? Will we be utilizing the matchlock guns from the Portuguese, my lord?" General Saasa asked.

"No. Save the tanegashima for the Takeda. They won't know what hit them," Nobunaga replied.

One Month Later – The Tenshō Iga War

The mountains of Iga Province had become a charnel house of systematic destruction. What had begun as a coordinated assault had evolved into a methodical campaign of annihilation that would echo through history as one of Nobunaga's most complete victories.

Southern Front - General Gamō Ujisato's Perspective:

The southern approach had proven the most challenging, with ninja forces using the rugged terrain to maximum advantage. Gamō's forces had advanced through narrow mountain passes where every shadow might conceal death, every cliff face a potential ambush point.

"They come like ghosts," one of his lieutenants had reported after the third day of fighting. "Kill two and five more appear from nowhere. As if from the shadows."

But the general had pressed forward with relentless determination. Against his better wishes—hopeful to preserve munitions—Nobunaga agreed to Gamō's ashigaru formations, to use arquebus matchlock to thin out the ninjas, as this tactic proved to be devastatingly effective against their signature sudden attacks. The thunderous roar of coordinated gunfire echoed through the mountains as black powder smoke drifted between the trees like fog.

Bodies littered the mountain paths—ninja in their dark clothing sprawled beside samurai in bloodied armor. The acrid smell of gunpowder mixed with the metallic stench of spilled blood filled the air as Gamō's forces systematically cleared each defensive position. By the end of the first month, the southern passes ran red with the evidence of Oda determination.

Northern Front - Nobukatsu's Proving Ground:

Young Nobukatsu had initially struggled with the psychological reality of command, but his samurai training had eventually surfaced and asserted itself. What he lacked in skill, he easily made up for it in bravery. Armed with a strong sense of his father's confidence, Nobukatsu unwaveringly led his forces head on with smooth calculated efforts, paying dividends. They had encountered lighter resistance on the northern approach, allowing him to build on his develop self-assurance while engaging manageable numbers of enemy fighters.

His blade work, while lacking his father's legendary skill, showed promise and steady improvement as he cut through the enemy. During one memorable engagement, he had personally out-dueled a ninja commander atop a mountain ridge, their swords ringing against each other as dawn broke over the blood-soaked landscape.

"For the honor of the Oda clan!" Nobukatsu had shouted as his blade found its mark, following a swift parry, sending his opponent tumbling into the ravine below. A smile splashed across his face as his troops had cheered with genuine enthusiasm, their respect for their young commander growing with each display of courage.

The northern front had become a proving ground where Nobukatsu learned to balance mercy with necessity, discovering that leadership in war required harder choices than he had imagined.

Eastern Front - Akechi's Arrow Storm:

Akechi had approached the campaign with cold, methodical precision that bordered on artistic in its efficiency. His legendary archery skills had become the stuff of battlefield legend as he systematically eliminated ninja attempting to flee the tightening noose.

From elevated positions, he would loose arrow after arrow with mechanical accuracy, each shaft finding its target with lethal precision. His quiver seemed inexhaustible as he cut down fleeing figures at distances that should have made accurate shooting impossible.

"Fifty-three confirmed kills," his aide had reported after one particularly productive day. "The men are calling you the 'Death Wind,' General."

But there was no joy in Akechi's efficiency, only the grim satisfaction of a man working through barely controlled rage. With each arrow he loosed, he imagined a different target—one much closer to home, one whose dark skin made him an easy mark even in the chaos of battle.

"The enemy is retreating, sire. Should I reload your quiver?" his aide asked.

"Yes. But save ten a few of the heavier ones. I'll need them for a later time," Akechi said with a grim smirk.

Western Front - Nobunaga and Yasuke's Command:

The western approach had been designated as the command position, allowing Nobunaga to coordinate the overall campaign while maintaining strategic flexibility. Yasuke had remained at his lord's side, serving as both bodyguard and tactical advisor as reports flowed in from the other fronts.

During the second month of fighting, their position had come under direct assault during a moonless night when a group of elite ninja had attempted to decapitate the Oda leadership. The attack had been sudden and nearly successful—shadowy figures appearing from the darkness with poisoned blades and throwing stars.

Yasuke's Kotegiri had sung through the night air as he intercepted attackers targeting Nobunaga. In a short time of welding his blade, Yasuke had developed an uncanny knack for deflecting projectiles such as stars and throwing knives, with unparalleled efficiency—occasionally repelling them back at their assailants. The shortened blade also proved perfect for the close-quarters combat, its edge cutting through ninja armor and flesh with equal ease. One by one ninja blood spilled around Yasuke with proficient swings as he carefully headed Nobunaga's training which preserved his energy for long squabbles.

Meanwhile, Nobunaga wielded his Heshikiri Hasebe with devastating effect, the legendary sword living up to its reputation by cutting through anything in its path. He drove it's sharp edge through countless ninja warriors, making them fall by what seemed as multitudes of ten to twenty in each battle.

As the fights waned on, there were too many close calls to count and thankfully, Yasuke proved to be exactly what Nobunaga needed—a trustworthy second set of eyes. "Behind you, my lord!" Yasuke had shouted, spinning to deflect a throwing star aimed at Nobunaga's back before his follow-up strike opened the attacker from sternum to spine. It wasn't until the attacker had withered to the ground before Nobunaga even knew what had transpired, pre-occupied with killing two others in his path. Thankful, he offered Yasuke a nod of gratitude before resuming the battle.

The ground around their command post had become slick with blood as they fought back-to-back, their contrasting fighting styles complementing each other perfectly. Nobunaga's precise, economical movements flowed seamlessly with Yasuke's more powerful, sweeping attacks. It was a sight to see, as occasionally on-looking Oda clan samurai found themselves doing more observation than fighting. Together, they were truly an uncompromising and deadly two headed snake, destined to overthrow any opposition in their path.

By dawn, forty or so ninja bodies lay scattered around their position, and neither commander had sustained serious injury.

The Final Assault:

After two months of systematic pressure from all directions, Iga's resistance had been reduced to a handful of strongholds centered around the mountain fortress of their leader, Momochi Sandayūa—legendary ninja master whose very name was whispered with fear throughout the province.

"The time has come," Nobunaga had announced during the final war council. "We end this today."

The assault on Momochi's stronghold had been a masterpiece of coordinated warfare. Arquebus formations had shattered the outer defenses while samurai units stormed the breached walls. Yasuke and Nobunaga had led the final charge personally, their legendary blades carving a path through the desperate defenders.

Momochi Sandayū had made his final stand in the fortress's highest tower, a figure draped in shadow and legend who seemed to embody the dying art of the ninja. His confrontation with Nobunaga had been brief but memorable—two masters of warfare meeting in single combat while the battle raged around them.

Momochi Sandayū had put up a good fight, but as fatigue got eh best of him, his hand froze to the sword and his dropped his guard, just long enough for Nobunaga to disarm him from the elbow down. "Your time is over, old man," Nobunaga had declared as Heshikiri Hasebe separated the ninja master's head from his shoulders with one decisive cut.

The fall of their leader had broken the remaining resistance. Within hours, the last of Iga's defenders had either fled into the deep mountains or submitted to Oda authority.

As the campaign concluded, the samurai had celebrated by burning the provincial temples and ninja training grounds—erasing centuries of tradition in a matter of hours. Smoke had risen from a dozen different fires as the Oda forces systematically eliminated any possibility of future rebellion.

Chants of, "Tenka-dono, Tenka-dono," echoed across the valley as the men acknowledged the well fought victory. Indeed, the Lord of the Realm was victorious.

The Journey Home

The return journey to Azuchi-jo had taken on the character of a victory parade, with captured banners and confiscated weapons serving as trophies of their success. Nobunaga and Yasuke rode at the head of the column, their conversation carrying the easy familiarity of warriors who had shared combat.

"You have fought with great honor, Yasuke-san," Nobunaga observed, his tone carrying genuine respect.

"Are campaigns always of such duration, Lord Nobunaga?" Yasuke asked, still processing the scale of what they had accomplished.

"Sometimes longer, sometimes shorter—only as long as necessary to complete our objectives. Proper planning makes the difference." Nobunaga gestured toward the long column of returning troops. "Initial reports from our strategic advisors indicate we eliminated approximately ten thousand ninja and local defenders. Some survivors even joined our forces upon surrender. We preserved roughly forty thousand of our own warriors."

"And your son, Nobukatsu?"

Nobunaga's expression showed paternal pride tempered with realistic assessment. "He performed... adequately. Better than expected for his first major command."

"Assigning him to the less heavily contested sector was wise strategy," Yasuke said.

"Experience is more valuable than any accolades he might have earned through premature heroics," Nobunaga replied. "He learned important lessons about leadership under pressure."

A shadow crossed Yasuke's features. "It is unfortunate that Nobutada was not present to witness this victory. I know he would have been proud to see his brother's development."

Nobunaga's jaw tightened slightly. "Yes. If not for his... actions, he would have been here to participate. Now he will understand the weight of consequences more clearly. Perhaps he will make better decisions in the future."

Yasuke nodded with a sigh. "Hopefully, he will have his opportunity for redemption, my lord."

"Hopefully, he will earn it," Nobunaga said with finality. "For now, we return to Azuchi-jo, regroup our forces, and resupply. Once we have had time to strategize our next moves, the Takeda clan will fall as completely as Iga Province."

Months Later – Early 1582

The late winter cold had settled over Azuchi-jo like a burial shroud, but within the war room, the atmosphere burned with anticipation. Snow dusted the paper screens while braziers provided warmth for the assembled generals as they planned what would become the final major campaign of Nobunaga's career.

"The past months have not only expanded our territory but rallied additional allies to our cause," General Sassa reported with evident satisfaction. "Our available forces now exceed fifty thousand warriors, with allied daimyo contributing additional support."

Maps of Takeda territory covered the table, marked with defensive positions, supply routes, and strategic objectives. The target was clear: Takatenjin Castle, the mountain fortress that served as the heart of Takeda power.

"Weather conditions favor rapid movement," General Niwa added. "The spring thaw will begin soon, but mountain passes remain accessible for coordinated assault. Our intelligence indicates Takeda Katsuyori has concentrated his remaining forces at the castle, making this a decisive engagement. Maybe now would be a good time to utilize the Portuguese matchlock guns, my lord."

"Perhaps." Nobunaga studied the tactical situation with the practiced eye of a master strategist. "Nobutada's forces in the eastern territories have been successful in disrupting Takeda supply lines. His campaigns have weakened their defensive capabilities significantly."

"The boy has learned from his mistakes," Akechi observed, his tone neutral but his eyes showing the calculation behind every word.

"Indeed," Nobunaga agreed. "It's settled then. This campaign will utilize our full combined-arms capabilities. Arquebus formations, cavalry charges, and traditional siege techniques. We will demonstrate the complete superiority of Oda military innovation."

Yasuke leaned forward to study the maps more closely. "The castle's position suggests they expect conventional siege tactics. Perhaps we should consider..."

"Yes?" Nobunaga prompted.

"Multiple simultaneous assaults from unexpected directions. If we can coordinate attacks on what appear to be impossibly difficult approaches, we might achieve the same surprise advantage that served us so well in Iga Province," Yasuke suggested.

"Excellent thinking," Nobunaga approved. "We move out in ten days."

A Moment of Peace

The evening before departure, Nobunaga had requested private time with his family—a rare luxury for a man whose life had been consumed by warfare for decades. The family quarters had been prepared with special care, elegant silk hangings and fresh flowers creating an atmosphere of domestic tranquility that felt almost foreign after months of military planning.

Following a decadent dinner meal fit for a shogunate, Lady Nōhime sat beside her husband with the grace and patience that had sustained their marriage through countless campaigns. Her dark hair was arranged in the formal style befitting her station, but her eyes showed the wear of a woman who had spent too many nights wondering if her husband would return from battle.

"You have been more patient than any man deserves," Nobunaga said softly, taking her hand in his.

"It goes without saying, that you are the daimyo, my love. You wear your new title well. Udaijin, Minister of the Right. You are to be respected, trusted, and revered, but most of all, honored. It is my duty," Lady Nōhime replied.

"I hope these years have not been wasted on duty only," Nobunaga said with a sly smile.

Lady Nōhime squeezed his hand tightly as she gazed into his eyes. "You know it is more than that, my love."

"When this campaign concludes successfully, I promise we will have time for peace." Nobunaga paused to momentarily regard his family gathered around him. His mind drifted to his past—filled with thoughts of the betrayal he experienced from those closest to him—and then to the present as he considered Nobutada. He turned to his wife. "Time to be a family again."

"I have learned to find contentment in the moments between wars," she replied with gentle wisdom. "But yes, I look forward to a time when your greatest concern is which garden to visit and which field to plow, not which enemy to defeat."

Before them, their children had gathered for the farewell—Nobukatsu still glowing with pride from his Iga Province success, young Nobutaka eager for his chance to prove himself in future campaigns, and their daughters maintaining the proper dignity expected of their station while their eyes showed concern for their father's safety. All that was missing was Nobutada and his absence was finally felt as Nobunaga fought back the unthinkable—that at any time, this moment could be his last with them all, as such are the risks of war.

"Take care of your mother while I'm gone," Nobunaga instructed his sons. "And remember—honor is earned through actions, not birthright."

The family moment had provided a brief respite from the weight of command, a reminder of what he fought to protect and preserve. Life was more than just rallying the nations of Japan as a unified country, but on a smaller level, keeping that which was entrusted to him—his family—safe.

The Takeda Campaign

The assault on Takeda territory had unfolded with the mechanical precision of a master craftsman's work. Nobunaga's forces had moved through the mountain approaches like an unstoppable tide, their combined-arms tactics proving devastatingly effective against traditional defensive positions. For some reason, their domination seemed more magical than conventional. Nobunaga couldn't help but consider that his reputation for dominance had preceded him at an ethereal level, which he himself could not fully understand, making those in opposition almost expectant of their demise.

The thunder of coordinated arquebus fire had echoed through mountain valleys as rotating firing lines maintained constant pressure on enemy positions. Each volley had sent dozens of Takeda defenders tumbling from their walls while clouds of black powder smoke drifted across the battlefield like incense from a funeral pyre.

During one particularly intense engagement outside Takatenjin Castle's outer defenses, Yasuke had found himself fighting alongside the very man he knew had murdered Ostrimyo.

Akechi Mitsuhide.

He had been positioned on a rocky outcrop, his legendary bow sending arrow after arrow into the ranks of charging Takeda samurai with mechanical precision.

A group of enemy warriors had managed to scale the cliff face behind Akechi's position, their approach masked by the chaos of battle. Yasuke had spotted the threat some time ago and when his screams to alert Akechi of their charge went unnoticed due to the deafening sound of gunfire and sword clatter, Yasuke took it upon himself to scale the wall faster than the attackers and personally deal with them.

Just as the lead attacker raised his sword to strike Akechi from behind, Kotegiri had moved with liquid grace, the legendary blade severing the attacker's arm before opening his throat in a single fluid motion. The other two assassins had fallen quickly to Yasuke's devastating combination of African martial arts and Japanese swordsmanship as he turned and sliced one in half, before rolling to his left to avoid an attack before plunging his sword deep into the heart of the other.

Akechi had turned to see the bodies scattered around his position, his expression showing surprise and something that might have been gratitude. Yasuke removed his blade from the body of the last assassin and wiped the blood clean from it with the crease of his elbow's sleeve. He looked up at Akechi and through narrowed eyes. But when their eyes met, Akechi couldn't find it in his heart to even acknowledge the feat. He simply turned back to his archery without a word.

The gesture had not gone unnoticed by other samurai, who began to whisper about the foreign warrior's honor in protecting even those who showed him no friendship.

The Battle of Temmokuzan

The final confrontation had taken place on the wind-swept plateau of Temmokuzan, where Takeda Katsuyori had made his desperate last stand with the remnants of his once-mighty clan. The battle had raged from dawn until late afternoon, with neither side giving ground easily.

Yasuke had fought beside Nobunaga throughout the engagement, their contrasting styles once again creating a deadly partnership that slashed through enemy ranks like a scythe through wheat. Nobunaga's Heshikiri Hasebe had lived up to its legendary reputation, cutting through armor and weapons with equal ease, while Yasuke's Kotegiri had continually proven equally devastating in close-quarters combat.

The tide had turned when Nobunaga's forces had managed to isolate Katsuyori from his remaining supporters. The Takeda leader had found himself surrounded, his options reduced to surrender or death.

"Please, Lord Nobunaga," Katsuyori had pleaded, falling to his knees with his hands extended in supplication. "You are the Dairokuten Maō. Consider sparing my life. My surviving troops and I could be valuable to your cause of total unification. If you show mercy, I promise that you will sit on the imperial throne one day. Perhaps with me serving loyally by your side." He had offered his hands in submission, his head bowed in apparent humility.

Nobunaga had studied the defeated daimyo with cold calculation before responding. "Your humility is... admirable. And you are right to fear me as the Demon King. As such, I acknowledge your submission. Unfortunately, that is all the honor you possess, and it is insufficient to atone for your past offenses against the Oda clan."

Heshikiri Hasebe had completed its arc before Katsuyori could raise his head, separating it from his shoulders in one clean cut that sent blood spraying across the mountain stone.

The psychological impact on the remaining Takeda forces had been immediate and total. Within minutes, organized resistance had collapsed as surviving warriors either fled into the mountains or submitted to Oda authority.

As the troops had begun salvaging weapons and valuables from the battlefield, something remarkable had occurred. The samurai who had witnessed Yasuke's performance throughout the campaign had begun gathering around him, their faces showing genuine respect and admiration.

"Yasuke! Yasuke! Yasuke!" The chant had started with a few voices but quickly spread through the ranks until hundreds of warriors were calling his name.

The foreign slave who had arrived at Azuchi-jo barely able to speak Japanese had transformed into a legendary samurai whose prowess was acknowledged by his peers. Nobunaga had watched the impromptu celebration with evident satisfaction, seeing his judgment vindicated by the warriors' spontaneous recognition.

But not everyone had joined the celebration.

Seeds of Treachery

Away from the main body of celebrating troops, Akechi had withdrawn with a small group of his most trusted retainers. The men gathered around him represented the core of his personal loyalty—warriors who had served under his command for years and whose allegiance to him superseded their obligation to the Oda clan.

Saitō Toshimitsu, his most senior lieutenant, had glanced nervously toward the continuing celebration. "The men seem genuinely impressed with the foreign warrior's abilities."

"Abilities," Akechi had spat, his composure finally cracking. "This inu is not Japanese, nor is he samurai by birth or breeding. I will not allow this farce to continue under my watch. Nobunaga has become intoxicated with his intrigue of this foreigner. His judgment is clouded. Owari Province and everything we have sacrificed to build it is indeed in grave danger."

Mizuno Katsunari, another longtime supporter, had shifted uncomfortably. "But what are we to do? Lord Nobunaga is our daimyo. We are bound by honor to follow his commands."

"As long as he reigns, we must obey his will," added Akechi Hidemitsu, Akechi Mitsuhide cousin, though his tone suggested reluctance rather than conviction.

Akechi had turned to face his conspirators directly, his eyes burning with an intensity that made several of them step backward involuntarily. "Then he will not be daimyo for much longer."

The words had hung in the mountain air like an executioner's blade, carrying implications that would reshape the history of Japan. In that moment, surrounded by the evidence of another Oda victory and the sound of his enemies celebrating a foreign warrior's success, Akechi Mitsuhide had crossed the line from loyal retainer to treasonous rebel.

The senso—the war—was about to take a turn that no one, not even Nobunaga himself, could have anticipated.

As the sun set over the bloodied battlefield of Temmokuzan, the shadows were already gathering for the event that would ultimately define both Yasuke's legend and Akechi's infamy.

Chapter 18: The Alɔŋ

LATE MAY 1582

The triumphant procession that wound its way through the gates of Azuchi-jo carried with it the electric energy of complete victory. The returning warriors bore their captured banners like sacred relics, while the sound of their voices echoed off the compound walls in a chant that had become both celebration and proclamation:

"Yasuke! Yasuke! Yasuke!"

The name rang through the air with such fervor that servants emerged from their quarters, farmers looked up from their fields, and children gathered to witness the return of the legendary foreign samurai. What had begun as recognition among the troops had evolved into something approaching worship among the common people of the domain.

From his position near the rear of the column, Akechi Mitsuhide watched the spectacle with barely concealed revulsion. Each repetition of that foreign name felt like a dagger twist in his gut, a reminder that everything he had worked for, everything he believed in, was being swept away by the enthusiasm of fools who couldn't see the danger they were celebrating.

Nobunaga had ordered a victory feast worthy of their achievements, and the great hall had been transformed into a scene of opulent celebration. Silk banners bearing the Oda mon hung alongside captured enemy standards, while tables groaned under the weight of delicacies and fine wine. The air filled with laughter, conversation, and the particular atmosphere of men who had faced death and emerged victorious.

As the evening progressed, a woman of exceptional beauty and evident experience entered the hall followed by a retinue of equally stunning companions. Okiku moved through the celebration with the practiced grace of one accustomed to serving the desires of powerful men, her silk robes and elaborate hair ornaments marking her as a courtesan of the highest caliber.

She approached Yasuke with obvious interest, having noted his elevated position and the respect shown him by the other warriors. "The great Yasuke-san," she said with a respectful bow. "Your reputation precedes you, even in my... profession."

"You honor me, Okiku-san," Yasuke replied politely.

"I must congratulate Lord Nobunaga on his recent appointment," she continued, gesturing toward where the daimyo held court. "Gondainagon—Honorary Major Counselor. Such recognition from the imperial court is well deserved."

"Indeed," Yasuke agreed. His eyes fell over Nobunaga as he spoke before landing back on the beautiful woman before him. "Lord Nobunaga's achievements speak for themselves."

As they spoke, Yasuke observed Nobunaga's interaction with his wife. The daimyo kissed Lady Nōhime tenderly before sending her away with gentle words—a ritual that Okiku noted with professional understanding. "He is a man of great appetites," she observed quietly. "Victory stirs the blood in ways that require... satisfaction. It is always thus when warriors return from campaign." She studied Yasuke with calculating eyes, and then cleared her throat. "What is your appetite, sir? You are a very large man—surely you would only be satisfied by two or three of my finest companions?"

Yasuke shook his head with gentle firmness. "I'm sorry to disappoint, but my heart belongs to another."

Okiku's expression shifted to one of patient understanding. "I respect that, truly. But your flesh needs to be fed just as much as your heart, if not more. The eyes, the mind, the senses—they all want what *they* want." As she spoke, she took his hand and placed it over the center of her breast, now making herself a personal offering with practiced seduction.

Yasuke slowly but firmly withdrew his hand. "As appealing as that sounds, my spirit and my soul are connected eternally to my bride. To the one whom my soul loves, I remain committed."

He bowed respectfully and made his exit, leaving Okiku with a mixture of surprise and admiration. From across the hall, Nobunaga observed Yasuke's departure, his own hand pausing with a cup of sake halfway to his lips, a few ladies women hung next to him, awaiting his attention. For a moment, something resembling contemplation crossed the daimyo's features as he considered his own behavior and choices.

The Next Morning

The war room felt different in the morning light—more serious, less celebratory than the previous evening's festivities. Nobunaga arrived to find Yasuke already present, standing at attention near the maps that still showed their recent conquests.

"Last night, Yasuke-san, you left the festivities rather prematurely, I'm afraid," Nobunaga observed with mild curiosity.

"I meant no disrespect, Lord Nobunaga. I was simply exhausted from our campaigns and felt it best to preserve my energy for more pressing matters—like protecting the province."

Nobunaga nodded with understanding. "As you should. Still, it's a pity. Every man must enjoy the spoils of war. Why else do we conquer as we do? Next time, I hope I don't have to command you to partake."

The comment carried a sly smile that suggested both amusement and genuine puzzlement at Yasuke's restraint. "You are daimyo, my lord," Yasuke replied diplomatically. "You do as you please."

The arrival of the other generals and advisors brought the informal conversation to an end, but the exchange had revealed something about both men that would prove significant in the hours to come.

As the council session began, reports flowed in regarding the aftermath of their Takeda victory. The numbers were impressive but concerning—while their strategic objectives had been achieved completely, the cost in manpower had been significant.

"We lost approximately eight thousand warriors across both campaigns," General Sassa reported soberly. "Additionally, we've left substantial garrison forces to maintain control of the conquered territories."

General Niwa leaned forward with evident concern. "This leaves our home defenses somewhat vulnerable. Perhaps we should recall some of the occupation forces to strengthen Azuchi-jo's protection."

Nobunaga waved dismissively. "Unnecessary. Our reputation alone provides adequate deterrent against potential threats. Besides, abandoning our gains to shore up defenses would signal weakness."

But several other generals voiced similar concerns, creating a chorus of opposition that clearly irritated their lord. It was then that Akechi chose to add his voice to the dissent. "My lord, I must agree with my colleagues," Akechi said with calculated boldness. "Our current position, while glorious, may be strategically unsound. We should consider—"

"Enough!" Nobunaga's voice cut through the discussion like a blade. "Why must I continue to be challenged by my own retainers? Consider Yasuke here—he does not question my authority, yet has become arguably the greatest warrior among our samurai. You could all learn from his example." The daimyo's gaze swept the assembled generals before settling on Yasuke. "As a matter of fact, Yasuke is now officially a general and my second in command."

A low hush spread across the room like ripples on a pond. Several generals shifted uncomfortably while others stared at Yasuke with expressions ranging from surprise to resentment. But it was Akechi's reaction that dominated the moment—he rose to his feet, his composure finally shattered completely. "My lord," Akechi said, his voice trembling with barely controlled fury, "this is madness. To elevate a foreign slave above samurai who have served the Oda clan for generations—"

"Careful, General," Nobunaga replied coldly. "You will address my second in command with appropriate respect, or you will face the consequences of insubordination."

Akechi's face had gone white with rage, his hands clenched into fists at his sides. The moment stretched like a bowstring pulled to its breaking point, with every man in the room sensing that they were witnessing something that would fundamentally alter the balance of power within the Oda hierarchy. "I will not serve under a barbarian," Akechi declared with finality.

The words hung in the air like incense smoke, carrying implications that everyone understood. Nobunaga's expression hardened into something approaching judicial pronouncement.

"Then you face a choice, General Akechi. Accept death for your insubordination, or accept banishment from my service."

For a heartbeat, it seemed that Nobunaga might actually order the execution of his longtime retainer. But something—perhaps old loyalty, perhaps sentiment—stayed his hand.

Immensely uncomfortable, Yasuke attempted to speak up. "My Lord—"

"Actually," Nobunaga continued with apparent magnanimity, "you will have one final opportunity to redeem yourself. Lead your troops to support Hashiba Hideyoshi at Takamatsu Castle. Perhaps serving under another commander will remind you of the value of loyalty."

Akechi bowed stiffly, his movements mechanical and filled with suppressed hatred. "As you wish, *Demon King*."

The title, spoken with such venom, carried implications that made several generals wince. Akechi turned on his heel and strode from the room without further ceremony, leaving behind an atmosphere thick with tension and unspoken questions.

Miles From Azuchi-Jo

The night air carried the sound of Akechi's war council like whispers between conspirators. His most trusted retainers had gathered around a small fire, their faces illuminated by flickering flames that cast dancing shadows across their features.

"The orders are clear," Akechi announced to the circle of loyal followers. "We will not be proceeding to Takamatsu Castle as commanded."

Saitō Toshimitsu looked up with obvious concern. "My lord, to disobey direct orders—"

"The orders come from a man whose judgment has been corrupted beyond redemption," Akechi cut him off. "Nobunaga's obsession with that foreign savage has blinded him to reality. The Oda clan—everything we have sacrificed to build—stands in mortal danger."

Mizuno Katsunari shifted uncomfortably. "What do you propose, General?"

Akechi's eyes burned with fanatic intensity as he outlined his plan. "We divide our forces. One contingent will move against Nobutada at Nijō Palace—we cannot allow the heir to escape and potentially rally opposition. While the main force returns to Azuchi-jo to deal with Nobunaga directly."

"This is treason," Akechi Hidemitsu whispered, though his tone suggested fascination rather than horror.

"Cousin, *this* is salvation," Akechi corrected. "When the dust settles, Japan will thank us for preserving it from the corruption of foreign influence."

The conspirators looked at each other with a mixture of fear and excitement. They were crossing a line from which there could be no return, but Akechi's conviction was infectious. One by one, they nodded their agreement.

"For the preservation of true Japanese values," Saitō said finally.

"For the honor of the samurai class," added Mizuno.

"For the future of Japan," Akechi concluded. "We move at dawn. It's time to end this nonsense and return the Azuchi-jo to its rightful place of respect and admonition. Without Ostrimyo, they'll never see us coming."

Several Day Later – Morning At Azuchi-Jo

The sun hung low on the horizon, painting the sky in shades of gold and crimson that seemed to promise either glory or doom depending on one's perspective. Yasuke had found Nobunaga on the palace balcony, the same spot where he had first been given his name and purpose.

"My lord," Yasuke began carefully, "I must speak with you about a matter of great concern."

Nobunaga turned from his contemplation of the sunset, noting the serious expression on his companion's face. "You seem troubled, Yasuke-san."

"I have been hearing rumors, my lord. The servant girls speak of strange movements, unusual activities. There are whispers of... unrest."

"What kind of unrest?"

Yasuke chose his words with extreme care. "Sometimes, the enemy from within is stronger and more deceptive than those outside, because you cannot see them coming. I fear for your safety, my lord."

Nobunaga's expression sharpened. "From whom specifically?"

"Akechi, my lord. I have observed things over time—details that seem to add up to suspicious behavior. I even have reason to believe that Ostrimyo's death was not the work of enemy ninja."

The accusation hung between them like an unsheathed blade. Nobunaga's reaction was immediate and defensive. "Nonsense," he huffed. "Akechi may be jealous, envious perhaps, but he has served me faithfully for ten years. He is not a traitor. Do you have proof of these accusations?"

"No, I'm afraid I don't," Yasuke admitted. "Only strong suspicion based on observation and instinct."

"Akechi and I have fought through many campaigns together, dating back to 1559 when we first secured Owari Province. He has demonstrated his loyalty time and again, even when I have been... less than admirable in my treatment of him."

Yasuke pressed forward despite Nobunaga's resistance. "Unfortunately, like the seasons, men change over time, Lord Nobunaga. Our troops are spread thin across the conquered territories. We don't have sufficient defenses here to ward off a determined attack. You need to recall Nobutada. You need your family close during these uncertain times."

The mention of family seemed to break through Nobunaga's defensive walls. His expression softened as he considered the implications of what Yasuke was suggesting. "You truly believe the danger is that immediate?"

"I believe a man who has lost everything learns to recognize the signs of approaching loss in others," Yasuke replied quietly. "I have been separated from my family for years, sold away from everything I held dear. I have learned to treasure the bonds that remain and to protect them fiercely."

Nobunaga studied Yasuke's face, noting the pain that flickered across his features. "Your wife and daughter—you speak of them so rarely."

"The pain of separation never lessens," Yasuke said, his hand unconsciously moving to touch the elephant-tusk pendant beneath his clothing. "Every sunrise reminds me of another day I cannot hold them, cannot protect them, cannot see my daughter grow into the woman she will become."

"And you fear I may face similar loss if I ignore your warnings."

"I fear that men like us—leaders, protectors—often sacrifice our families for our ambitions without realizing it until it's too late," Yasuke replied. "You have children who love you, a wife who has waited through countless campaigns. Don't let pride cost you what truly matters."

The two men stood in companionable silence, watching the sun sink toward the horizon. Both were warriors who had lost much in pursuit of honor and duty, both fathers separated from their children by the demands of their stations.

"You know," Nobunaga said quietly, "there are times when I wonder if my father felt this same weight—this constant choice between family and duty."

"The difference is that you still have the chance to choose both," Yasuke observed. "Call Nobutada home. Gather your family close. Face whatever comes with those you love beside you."

Nobunaga nodded slowly, the wisdom of the advice overriding his initial resistance. "Very well. I will send word immediately." He turned toward the palace interior, then paused. "Tomorrow, we journey to Honnō-ji Temple. It seems I have some work to do. Sunanomi will know how to locate Nobutada quickly. Tell him his young lord is needed... home."

As Nobunaga disappeared into the palace, Yasuke remained on the balcony, watching the last light fade from the sky. Somewhere in the gathering darkness, he sensed that forces were moving—forces that would test everything they had built and everything they held dear.

The alɔŋ was coming. The darkness was almost upon them.

But for now, in this moment of calm before the storm, he had done what he could to protect the man who had given him purpose, identity, and honor. Whether it would be enough remained to be seen.

The elephant pendant felt warm against his chest as night fell over Azuchi-jo, carrying with it the weight of prophecy and the promise of a reckoning that had been years in the making.

Chapter 19: The Muhon

JUNE 21, 1582 - HONNŌ-JI TEMPLE, KYOTO

The ancient Buddhist temple of Honnō-ji sat like a jewel in the heart of Kyoto, its weathered wooden structures and carefully tended gardens speaking to centuries of spiritual contemplation. What had once been a place of pure meditation had become a temporary headquarters for Nobunaga's political meetings with court officials and allied daimyo—an ironic transformation that would soon prove prophetic.

Yasuke stood guard in the main courtyard, his imposing figure a stark contrast to the peaceful monks who moved silently between the buildings. The small retinue that had accompanied Nobunaga to Kyoto was sufficient for normal diplomatic purposes, but something in the morning air felt different—charged with an electricity that reminded him of the moments before lightning struck.

It was then that Sunanomi arrived, his horse lathered with sweat from hard riding and his face bearing the urgency of crucial news.

Nijō Palace - Earlier That Morning

The reunion between Sunanomi and Nobutada had been electric with emotion and barely suppressed longing. After months of separation, seeing each other again felt like emerging from winter into spring. They had embraced longer than propriety strictly allowed, both men acutely aware of how much they had missed not just each other's presence, but the understanding that existed between them.

"Great Nobutada-sama," Sunanomi had said, his cheeks flushing as he delivered his message, "I bring urgent news from your father."

Nobutada's expression immediately shifted to concern. "Is he ill? Injured?"

"No, my lord. He has requested your immediate return to Azuchi-jo. The situation has become... delicate."

Recognizing the need for privacy, Nobutada had dismissed his men and led Sunanomi to his private quarters. Once the door was secured, the formal pretense had melted away as Nobutada cupped Sunanomi's face in his hands and kissed him with a passion that spoke of months of separation and longing.

"I've missed you," Nobutada whispered against Sunanomi's lips, his voice thick with emotion.

Sunanomi returned the kiss before gently separating, his duty overriding his desire. "My lord, you need to take your father's request seriously. There are rumblings of an impending attack on the compound."

Nobutada stepped back, his strategic mind immediately engaged. "From whom? Our enemies are nearly vanquished. My forces have eliminated the remaining Takeda strongholds at Kofu and Shinpu, and cleared out the mountain bandits who were using their territory as sanctuary. I've heard reports that Yasuke has been instrumental in Father's recent victories against the Buddhist militant factions. Surely the Oda clan's dominance is unquestioned by now."

"Yes, my lord, but this threat may come from within," Sunanomi said carefully. "There are whispers of internal discord among the generals. Many are deeply unhappy with your father's elevation of Yasuke. Making him a bodyguard was controversial, but promoting him to samurai status and now to general has crossed a line that many Japanese nobles cannot accept. Any one of them could attempt a coup."

Nobutada's face darkened. "To even speak of such treachery—"

"I know, my lord. I would never voice such concerns openly, only to you. I haven't even discussed this with Yasuke, as security has been much tighter since..." He paused meaningfully.

"The Wing's death."

"His murder, my lord."

Nobutada began pacing the room with the same restless energy that characterized his father's thinking process. Sunanomi watched with fond recognition, noting how the young lord's mannerisms increasingly reflected those of the daimyo.

"You are growing more like your father every day," Sunanomi observed, coming up behind Nobutada and embracing him gently. "Not just in reputation, but in how you carry yourself."

"How so?"

"This pacing. It has Lord Nobunaga written all over it."

Nobutada smiled despite his concerns. "Does he speak of me often when I'm away?"

"Not often, but I try to read his expression when reports of your successes arrive. As you know, your father is... difficult to interpret."

"Don't I know it." Nobutada turned in Sunanomi's arms. "When will you return with news of my departure?"

Sunanomi's expression grew troubled. "You're not leaving immediately?"

"My men have just returned from extensive raids throughout the former Takeda territories. They're exhausted and need rest. I know Father wants to see me, but my responsibility is to their welfare first."

"But what about the coup threat?"

Nobutada cupped Sunanomi's shoulders reassuringly. "There's no concrete evidence of such a plot. Father can protect himself—he has Yasuke now. Once my men have recovered, I'll return home. I promise."

He kissed Sunanomi once more before stepping back into his role as commander. "Return to Father quickly. Tell him I'll depart within three days. I have much to share about our recent victories."

Miles From Kyoto

In a secluded valley where ancient pines provided cover from observation, Akechi Mitsuhide sat astride his war horse, surveying the army he had assembled through careful planning and passionate persuasion. Nearly thirteen thousand warriors had answered his call—men who shared his belief that Japan's traditional values were under assault from foreign corruption.

The morning mist clung to the assembled banners as Akechi addressed his commanders one final time. His voice carried the fervor of a man who believed he was saving his nation from destruction. "Today, we reclaim Japan from the pollution that threatens to destroy everything our ancestors built," he declared. "The enemy awaits at Honnō-ji!"

The phrase would echo through history, but in that moment it carried the weight of absolute conviction. These men believed they were patriots, not traitors, and that conviction made them infinitely more dangerous than mere mercenaries.

As the army began its march toward Kyoto, Akechi felt the satisfaction of a plan years in the making finally reaching fruition. Everything that had built his resentment—the agricultural successes, the military victories, the insults of his family, the elevation of a foreign slave above Japanese nobility—would be answered today.

Honnō-Ji Temple – Late Afternoon

The afternoon sun streamed through the paper screens of Nobunaga's temporary quarters as he and Yasuke reviewed reports from their various campaigns. The peaceful atmosphere of the temple provided a stark contrast to the war rooms and battlefields that had dominated their recent months.

It was then that Nobunaga did something completely unexpected. "Yasuke-san," he began, his tone carrying an unusual formality, "there is a matter we must address. I have decided to elevate you to the rank of full commander of my personal forces."

Yasuke bowed respectfully. "You honor me, Lord Nobunaga."

"But that is not all." Nobunaga stood and moved to the window, looking out at the temple gardens where monks tended their eternal routines. "I must also apologize for something that has weighed on my conscience." The words hung in the air like incense smoke. Yasuke had never heard his lord apologize for anything. "I am sorry I have enslaved you for so long," Nobunaga continued, his voice heavy with genuine regret. "This practice of owning human beings is not truly Japanese in spirit. It corrupts both the master and the servant. I will free the remaining slaves in my domain, but first..." He turned to face Yasuke directly. "If you vow to protect this realm and its people, you will have the complete freedom you have sought for so long."

Yasuke felt the world shift around him. After years of dreaming of this moment, it arrived with such suddenness that he could barely process its reality. "My lord, I..." he began, and then stopped to gather his thoughts. "I vow to protect Japan and its people as if they were my own family. This land has given me purpose, identity, and honor. I will defend it with my life."

Nobunaga nodded solemnly. "Then we will seal this with the African blood oath you once told me about—a bond that cannot be revoked or broken."

Using a small ceremonial knife, both men cut their palms and clasped hands, allowing their blood to mingle while speaking words of eternal loyalty and mutual respect. In that moment, the last chains of slavery fell away, replaced by bonds of chosen brotherhood.

"You are no longer my slave, my servant, or even my retainer," Nobunaga declared. "You are my brother in arms, free to choose your own path."

The ceremony was interrupted by urgent shouts from the courtyard. Yasuke moved to the window and saw Sunanomi arriving with obvious distress, but before he could report, the evening air was shattered by war cries and the thunder of approaching horses.

The Assault Begins

The attack came with the coordinated precision of a military operation planned down to the smallest detail. Akechi's forces had surrounded the temple complex under cover of darkness, cutting off all escape routes before announcing their presence with a rain of fire arrows that set the outer buildings ablaze.

Yasuke's small force of retainers fought valiantly, but they were vastly outnumbered and caught completely off guard. The temple's peaceful courtyards became battlegrounds as monks fled in terror while samurai clashed in desperate combat.

Throughout the night, Yasuke led a fighting retreat through the burning complex, trying to buy time for reinforcements that he increasingly realized would never come. Each defensive position was eventually overrun, forcing them deeper into the temple's inner sanctum. Nobunaga had fled deeper into the interior while Yasuke held off as many attackers as he could.

As dawn approached, Yasuke found himself making a final stand in the main hall, the ancient wooden beams groaning overhead as flames consumed the centuries-old structure. It was then that he received confirmation of his worst fears.

"My lord," one of his surviving retainers gasped as he stumbled into the hall, "many of our own men have joined the attack against us. They wear Akechi's mon alongside their own."

The betrayal was complete. Not only had Akechi turned against his sworn lord, but he had convinced other samurai that their cause was just.

Yasuke finally found Nobunaga in his quarters, the daimyo's face reflecting a mixture of sorrow and grim acceptance. "Let me guess," Nobunaga said quietly, "there has been no word from my son?"

"No, my lord. The roads have been cut. No messengers can get through."

Nobunaga nodded as if he had expected this answer. "And Akechi?"

"Leading the assault personally."

"Then you were right, my friend. The enemy within proved more dangerous than any we faced in open battle." Nobunaga's voice carried no anger, only profound sadness as his eyes filled with tears. "I should have listened to your warnings."

"There may still be time to break through their lines," Yasuke suggested desperately.

"No." Nobunaga's voice was firm. Something deep down inside of him tore free. Whatever ideal of family—not that of blood—he held for Akechi had been forcefully ripped away with the actions of the day. "Take the remaining men and establish a defensive position in the main vestibule. You can funnel their forces there and perhaps hold them long enough for Nobutada to arrive."

"My lord—"

"That is an order, Commander Yasuke. And remember—you are a free man now and forever. Whatever happens to me, that cannot be taken away."

The Final Confrontation

The vestibule of Honnō-ji's inner temple had become a bottleneck of death. Yasuke and his handful of remaining warriors had positioned themselves to force Akechi's superior numbers into a narrow killing ground, but their ammunition and strength were nearly exhausted.

It was then that the arrows came.

The first shaft whistled through the smoky air straight toward Yasuke's head. Without thinking, he snatched it from the air with his left hand, the motion as fluid as breathing. Three more arrows followed in quick succession, and each one was deflected by precise movements of his katana—Kotegiri Masamune.

Yasuke sheathed his blade and stood tall, peering into the smoke-filled darkness of the adjacent corridors. His voice carried across the burning temple with absolute confidence. "Too bad for you, Akechi, that it will be much harder to kill a man who is not blind or drunk with sake."

The reference to Ostrimyo's murder hung in the air like an accusation until Akechi finally stepped from the shadows with his bow still in hand, flanked by a dozen of his most loyal retainers. "So the foreign dog finally shows his teeth," Akechi sneered. "You should have died that first morning when I saw you in your slave quarters. I should've ended you countless times after that."

"Funny, though. I count an even score between us. Or did you forget that last defeat in which I voluntarily offered you the chance to kill me?"

"Truc. And I should have taken you up on that. Maybe we would not be here today, in these conditions. Still, I do feel some gratification in this moment because tonight, you will not be so lucky as to receive my mercy. Although, I do feel like I already killed a part of you anyway, the moment I put an arrow through the old man's heart."

The confession hit Yasuke like a physical blow—harder than any lash from a whip he'd ever felt before as a slave—confirming what he had long suspected but could never prove. "You murdered the Wing," he replied, sounding more like a affirmation than an accusation.

"I eliminated an obstacle to Japan's purity," Akechi corrected. "Just as I am about to eliminate you."

Yasuke drew the Kotegiri, its edge gleaming in the firelight. "I am more of a samurai than you will ever be, because I have the one thing you lack—honor."

Akechi snickered. "A touching sentiment. Perhaps something for the history books. But no one will ever know or hear of it because you'll be dead by the end of the night."

"That's acceptable." Yasuke pointed his blade directly at Akechi's heart. "A very wise man—the one you murdered—once said that 'even in betrayal and death, honor must be preserved.' And that honor will be preserved by your severed head!"

Akechi gestured dismissively to his men. "Kill the rest. Leave the foreign devil to me."

As his retainers charged toward Yasuke's remaining defenders, Akechi drew his own katana and advanced with the confidence of a master swordsman who had never met his equal.

What followed was a duel that embodied everything their conflict had represented—tradition versus change, jealousy versus honor, hatred versus loyalty. Their blades met in a symphony of steel that rang through the burning temple like a funeral dirge.

Akechi put Yasuke's agility to the test, as the powerful African executed precision rolls and cartwheels at just the precise moment that the general would swing or slice, narrowly escaping the wrath of his blade. And when Yasuke had moments to counter, he made good with landing punches or kicks, in absence of an opportunity to pierce cold steel into flesh. Patience it seemed, would be the most valuable asset tonight.

Yasuke knew that Akechi was skilled, perhaps more skilled than any opponent he'd ever faced, and one false move would certainly end in his demise. All the teachings from Nobunaga, Ostrimyo, and Nobutada had prepared him for this moment. He would have to make good on his opportunities if he was to protect all that had been entrusted to him.

Aside from Akechi's seasoned swordplay, there was something else at hand that made him sinisterly dangerous, but it could possibly be exploited as well—his hatred for Yasuke. It made him reckless. Every strike carried too much emotion; every combination was colored by years of built up resentment and frustration. Yasuke regarded the slight, momentary delays that followed Akechi's wild strikes, as the unhinged general attempted to reset his defensive stance. Yasuke took note, anticipating the moment the fight would sway in his favor.

As the fight waned, Yasuke held his form and fought with the controlled fury of righteous vengeance. Every lesson from Ostrimyo held true before him, while each technique learned from Nobunaga took form, molding to his fighting style like an impressive kata. Every instinct honed through years of survival came together in a display of martial artistry that was both beautiful and terrible. And it was all he needed.

The end came suddenly.

Akechi overcommitted to a thrust that should have been fatal, but Yasuke's African martial arts training allowed him to flow around the attack like water around stone. The words of Ostrimyo echoed in his mind—piercing through time and space—exposing the advantage he sorely had been waiting for. 'Sway in the wind'—he heard the old man's voice utter as his body twisted sideways in a perfect execution of the Twin Blade technique. Akechi recoiled and let our a growl as he attempted one last wild, downward strike that would've ended most warriors.

But his was a samurai like no other.

In an instant, Nobunaga's training came to light as the words 'wait, parry, strike,' filled Yasuke's mind as his body perfectly mimicked its instructions. The Kotegiri moved with liquid grace, and suddenly Akechi was screaming as his right arm fell to the temple floor, severed cleanly at the forearm.

Akechi collapsed, clutching the bleeding stump where his sword hand had been, his face white with shock and agony. Yasuke stood over him with his blade raised for the killing stroke, but then stopped. Instead, he picked up Akechi's fallen katana and threw it down beside the defeated general. "Do what is honorable," Yasuke commanded, then turned away to seek his lord.

Behind him, Akechi stared at the blade through tears of pain and humiliation, understanding that even in defeat, his enemy had shown more honor than he had displayed in victory.

The Final Farewell

When Yasuke finally fought his way through the burning corridors to Nobunaga's quarters, he found the doors barricaded from within. Using his shoulder, he smashed through the wooden barrier to discover a scene that would haunt him forever.

Nobunaga knelt in the center of the room in formal seiza position, his wakizashi buried deep in his abdomen. Three enemy soldiers lay dead around him, evidence that he had fought to the end before choosing his final act.

Yasuke cut down two more attackers as he rushed to his lord's side, dropping to his knees beside the dying daimyo.

"My lord, why?" Yasuke whispered, his voice breaking with emotion.

Nobunaga's eyes, already growing dim, focused on Yasuke's face with effort. "Because... a leader must choose... his own ending." Blood flecked his lips as he spoke. "Yasuke... my brother... promise me..."

"Anything, my lord."

"Protect Nobutada... when he returns. Help him... rebuild what I have... broken." Nobunaga's hand found Yasuke's arm with failing strength. "You are... truly free now. Use that freedom... wisely."

Tears streamed down Yasuke's face as he held his dying lord. "I promise. I will find your son and tell him of your honor."

Nobunaga smiled faintly. "The mwali... serves his... true purpose..."

With those last words, the light faded from Nobunaga's eyes, leaving Yasuke alone with his grief in the burning temple.

Escape

The sound of approaching footsteps reminded Yasuke that his own survival was far from assured. Akechi's forces would want to eliminate all witnesses to their treachery, and a foreign samurai would be a particular prize.

With infinite gentleness, he closed Nobunaga's eyes and arranged his body in a position of dignity. Then, honoring his promise to survive and protect Nobutada, he sheathed his katana and prepared for escape.

The main corridors were blocked by enemy forces and the flames from the assault were slowly closing in, making it nearly impossible to find a safe route of escape. Suddenly, a bright light beamed in through a sliver in the paper screen of the walls, seemingly coming from the moon itself. There it was, a weakness in the temple's pristine architecture provided an alternative.

Yasuke charged toward the large paper screen that overlooked the courtyard pond, his powerful frame smashing through the wooden frame as arrows whistled past his head. He plunged into the cold water twenty feet below, the impact driving him deep beneath the surface. When he emerged, gasping and swimming toward the far shore, more arrows splashed around him, but the darkness and smoke provided cover for his escape.

Dragging himself from the pond, Yasuke looked back once at the burning temple where his lord had died and his own destiny had been forever changed. Then he disappeared into the forest, carrying with him his sword, the knowledge of what had transpired, and the responsibility to see that justice was eventually served.

Behind him, Honnō-ji burned like a funeral pyre, its flames visible for miles as they consumed not just ancient wood and paper, but an entire era of Japanese history.

The muhon was complete. The age of Nobunaga was over.

Chapter 20: The Athɔ̈m

The forest path leading away from the burning ruins of Honnō-ji was treacherous in the pre-dawn darkness, but Yasuke pressed forward with desperate urgency. A masterless horse, its samurai rider fallen in the battle, had provided him with the means to honor Nobunaga's final request. The animal's hooves thundered against the earthen road as Yasuke drove it mercilessly toward Nijō Palace, his heart heavy with the weight of promises that might already be broken.

The castle appeared through the morning mist like a vision from a more peaceful time, its elegant architecture and manicured gardens a stark contrast to the violence that had consumed the night. But even from a distance, Yasuke could see that something was terribly wrong. Smoke rose from several points within the complex, and the distinctive banners of Akechi's forces flew alongside captured Oda standards.

His worst fears were being realized.

Yasuke dismounted at the forest edge and approached on foot, using the ornamental gardens for cover as he surveyed the scene. Akechi's samurai moved through the palace grounds with the methodical efficiency of conquerors, systematically looting the treasures that had made Nijō Palace renowned throughout Japan.

They carried ancient scrolls bearing the calligraphy of master poets, delicate ceramic tea vessels that had been crafted by legendary artisans, and silk screens painted with scenes of natural beauty that had taken months to complete. Golden Buddha statues disappeared into silk wrappings while jade figurines and precious incense burners were catalogued for transport. The very soul of

Japanese artistic achievement was being stripped away piece by piece.

Using the chaos as cover, Yasuke made his way toward the inner palace where he knew Nobutada would have made his final stand. Each step felt like walking through a graveyard of dreams, the beauty around him tainted by the knowledge of what he would likely find.

The inner sanctuary maintained its serene elegance even in the midst of catastrophe. Sliding panels depicting cranes in flight still separated chambers where centuries of tea ceremonies had been conducted, while gardens visible through open screens continued their eternal cycles regardless of human tragedy.

It was in the main reception hall that Yasuke found him.

Nobutada knelt in formal seiza position in the center of the room, his wakizashi buried deep in his abdomen, his hands still maintaining perfect form even in death. Unlike his father's chaotic final moments, Nobutada's seppuku had been performed with meticulous attention to ritual and honor.

Yasuke rushed to his side, gathering the young lord's still-warm body into his arms as the last traces of life flickered in his eyes.

"Majok..." Nobutada whispered, using the name that carried with it the memory of their first meeting, their training sessions, their conversations about honor and family and the weight of inheritance.

The sound of his old name hit Yasuke like a physical blow, bringing with it a flood of memories—the shy young lord who had first invited him to spar, the growing friendship built through shared combat and mutual respect, the conversations about fathers and duty and the courage to choose one's own path.

"My lord," Yasuke whispered, his voice breaking with emotion as he held the dying man. "I promised your father I would protect you."

"You... did," Nobutada managed, his breath growing shallow. "You... gave me... the strength to... choose honor."

With those words, the light faded from Nobutada's eyes, leaving Yasuke alone with his grief and the weight of a world that had crumbled around him. The Oda clan—the family that had given him purpose, identity, and meaning—was gone. Everything he had fought to protect had been reduced to corpses and ashes.

The sound of heavy footsteps shattered his mourning. A group of samurai burst through the chamber doors, surrounding him with drawn swords as their leader emerged from behind the wall of steel.

Akechi Mitsuhide stepped forward, his right arm bound in a crude tourniquet and sling, his face pale from blood loss but his eyes burning with triumphant malice. "So the inu runs away, only to face the inevitable," Akechi sneered, raising a katana awkwardly with his remaining hand.

Yasuke gently laid Nobutada's body down and rose to face his tormentor, but something had broken inside him. The fire that had sustained him through years of slavery, training, and battle had been extinguished by the sight of Nobutada's lifeless form.

Akechi drove his blade downward, planting it in the wooden floor inches from Yasuke's feet—a gesture of dominance and contempt. Then, with deliberate cruelty, he reached out and stripped the ivory elephant pendant from around Yasuke's neck.

"Like I told you before, you are not a genuine samurai," Akechi declared, holding the mwali up to catch the morning light. "You do not deserve death by the sword, nor are you worthy of seppuku.

You are a foreign animal, nothing more." He gestured to his men with his good arm. "Take this maggot to the docks."

The soldiers rushed forward with iron shackles, and for the first time since his arrival in Japan, Yasuke offered no resistance. Dejected, drained, and broken by loss, he allowed them to bind his hands and drag him away from the bodies of the only family he had known.

As the chains locked around his wrists, he understood with bitter clarity that he was a free man no longer.

One Week Later

The cargo ship that had carried Yasuke from Japan creaked and groaned as it settled against the dock in the Italian port of Livorno. The journey had passed in a haze of grief and despair, the other human cargo—mostly prisoners of war and debtors—maintaining the silence of the damned.

When the ship's hold opened and the captives were herded onto dry land, Yasuke moved with the mechanical precision of a man whose spirit had been broken. The Mediterranean sun felt alien on his skin after the mists of Japan, and the foreign voices around him created a cacophony that reminded him how far he had fallen from grace.

It was then that a younger man approached, his clothing similar to the Jesuit robes that Yasuke remembered from his first encounters with European missionaries. The stranger moved with purpose through the crowd of newly arrived slaves, his eyes searching until they fixed on Yasuke's distinctive height and bearing.

"This way, brother," the man said in accented English, gently taking hold of Yasuke's wrist restraints.

Too exhausted to resist or question, Yasuke followed the stranger through the narrow streets of the port city to a modest stone building that served as both residence and workshop. The interior was simple but clean, with religious iconography sharing wall space with tools and ledgers that spoke of honest labor.

The young man produced a key and carefully removed Yasuke's shackles before gesturing to a simple wooden table set with bread, cheese, and wine. "Please, eat. You must be hungry after such a journey."

Yasuke sat but made no move toward the food. "What am I doing here?"

"Whatever you wish to do," the man replied with gentle sincerity. "You were purchased at considerable expense, and now your freedom is assured. You can work here with me and make an honest living, or you can leave to work the land on your own terms. The choice is entirely yours."

"Who are you?"

"My name is Leonardo Valignano. My father died two years ago, but he made me swear an oath that if you ever came to these shores, I would complete his promise and secure your freedom." Leonardo sat across from Yasuke, his expression earnest. "I went to the docks every day after his death, reading ship manifests and hoping you would arrive—Yasuke, the man once known as Majok. Your accomplishments in Japan became legendary to most. I had almost given up hope until today." He paused, a strange expression crossing his features. "I was resting in my chambers when an unfamiliar voice whispered to me: 'The prize awaits.' I knew it wasn't God—at least not the one I serve—but I felt compelled to investigate. It was as if fate itself was knocking at my door." Leonardo paused again, as if awaiting a response from Yasuke.

"Go on," Yasuke muttered.

Leonardo's eyes showed both determination and uncertainty. "Purchasing your freedom cost me nearly everything I have, so it would be wonderful if you stayed to help me recover the debt. But I would understand if you chose otherwise."

For the first time in days, Yasuke felt something stir within him—not hope exactly, but a flicker of possibility. "My family... I need to return to India to find them."

"Certainly," Leonardo nodded. "But we are in Italy now, and such a journey requires substantial resources. We occasionally face raiders in this region, and a man of your evident martial skills would be invaluable in protecting our community. Between farming my mill and providing security, you could earn passage to India relatively quickly."

Yasuke looked at the young man's earnest face and recognized something of his father's missionary zeal tempered with genuine compassion. For the first time since leaving Japan, he allowed himself to consider a future beyond mere survival.

"I will stay," he said simply.

Months Later

The work had been good for Yasuke's soul, if not his spirit. Physical labor in Leonardo's grain mill provided structure to his days, while occasional conflicts with bandits allowed him to maintain his fighting skills. Leonardo proved to be good company—intelligent, hardworking, and blessed with his father's gift for seeing the humanity in all people.

On this particular evening, they worked together loading sacks of grain onto pack horses for transport to a neighboring village. The routine had become comfortable, almost peaceful, and Yasuke found himself thinking more frequently about the future he might build in India when he had earned sufficient passage money.

"You've become quite the miller," Leonardo observed with obvious satisfaction. "Father would be pleased to see how well you've adapted to honest labor."

Yasuke secured the last of the grain sacks and mounted his horse. "Your father was a good man. His faith in redemption was... not misplaced."

As they prepared to depart, bright light suddenly erupted across the horizon. Fires bloomed throughout the village like deadly flowers, accompanied by the unmistakable sounds of violence and terror.

"Raiders!" Leonardo shouted.

Without hesitation, Yasuke dumped his grain sacks and spurred his horse toward the chaos. As he closed the distance to the village, he drew the saber that Leonardo had provided—a functional weapon that lacked the legendary quality of Kotegiri but served its purpose well enough.

The raiders were numerous but poorly disciplined, more accustomed to terrorizing farmers than facing trained opposition. Yasuke carved through their ranks with devastating efficiency, his years of training under Ostrimyo and Nobunaga evident in every movement. Eight men fell before they realized they faced a true warrior rather than another helpless villager.

But an arrow soon found Yasuke's horse, sending him tumbling to the ground. Yasuke's agility paid dividends as he swiftly and smoothly rolled to his feet and continued his assault on foot. The raiders' sloppy technique and lack of coordination made them easy prey for someone trained in the deadly arts of the samurai.

The tide of battle turned decisively in his favor as he systematically reduced their numbers. Leonardo appeared at his side, using a simple hand dagger to dispatch a raider who had attempted to attack Yasuke from behind. The two men shared a brief smile of triumph at their successful defense of the village.

It was then that a final raider emerged from the shadows behind Leonardo.

The blade opened Leonardo's throat before either man could react. Yasuke's scream of rage echoed across the burning village as he plunged through the remaining attackers, his saber finding flesh and bone with mechanical precision until no enemies remained standing.

In the sudden silence that followed, Yasuke surveyed the carnage around him. Bodies littered the village square—raiders and villagers alike. The fires continued to burn, consuming homes and workshops with equal hunger. As the reality of the situation settled over him, he realized that everyone was dead. Every single person who might have provided work, companionship, or the means to earn passage to India had been slaughtered.

His chances of ever returning to his family had died with Leonardo's last breath.

Yasuke screamed, the sound carrying all the anguish of a man who had lost everything not once, but repeatedly. He tore at his clothing in grief, his massive frame shaking with sobs as the weight of endless loss finally overwhelmed him.

His hand found the saber's hilt, and with sudden, terrible clarity, he understood what he had to do. There was nothing left—no purpose, no hope, no reason to continue an existence that brought nothing but pain to himself and death to those around him.

Raising the blade over his head, Yasuke prepared to join Leonardo, Nobutada, Nobunaga, and Ostrimyo in whatever realm awaited the dead. The steel felt cold against his skin as he positioned it carefully, determined to complete the seppuku that Akechi had denied him.

The blade plunged into his abdomen with surprising ease. He dropped to his knees, and then fell forward onto the weapon, driving it deeper as his life began to ebb away. The pain was sharp but brief, quickly replaced by a spreading numbness that promised peace.

As his eyes began to dim, however, something impossible appeared before him.

A large vortex materialized in the air above the burning village, its edges shimmering and pulsating with an otherworldly energy that hurt to look at directly. The portal seemed to exist outside normal reality, neither entirely there nor completely absent.

From within the swirling darkness came a voice—gentle but unfamiliar, speaking his name with an authority that transcended mortal understanding. "Yasuke..."

He tried to respond but found his voice had abandoned him along with his strength. The sight of the vortex filled him with a mixture of wonder and terror as he struggled to comprehend what he was witnessing.

The vortex slowly closed in on Yasuke as his body began to betray him with feelings of lifelessness overwhelming him. As his vision continued to fade, a small, beastly hand emerged from the portal—not human, but something far older and more powerful. The appendage was covered in scales that reflected the firelight like black mirrors, and its claws were longer than sword blades.

The beastly hand reached out and grasped Yasuke's weakening form, dragging him along the ground inexorably toward the swirling vortex. As consciousness finally abandoned him, he felt himself being pulled into a realm beyond mortal understanding, where the laws of death and life held no dominion.

Behind him, the village continued to burn, but Yasuke was no longer part of that world.

His story in the realm of mortals had reached its athӭm.

But somewhere beyond the veil of reality, another chapter was about to begin.

THE END?

EPILOGUE

The events that transpired at Honnō-ji temple on June 21, 1582, marked not merely the end of Oda Nobunaga's life, but the conclusion of an era that had fundamentally transformed Japan. When the flames finally died and the smoke cleared from Kyoto's ancient temple grounds, the man who had controlled approximately one-third of Japan lay dead by his own hand, his vision of unification seemingly destroyed alongside his mortal form.

Akechi Mitsuhide's triumph proved as ephemeral as morning mist. Despite his careful planning and passionate conviction that he was saving Japan from foreign corruption, his rule lasted a mere thirteen days. This brief period, which history would remember as "The Thirteen Days of the Demon King," came to an abrupt end when Toyotomi Hideyoshi—another of Nobunaga's loyal generals—defeated Akechi at the Battle of Yamazaki. The traitorous general's dreams of purging Japan of foreign influence died with him on that battlefield, his severed head a testament to the ultimate price of treachery.

Nobunaga's legacy, however, proved far more enduring than his enemies had anticipated. Though he never claimed the title of Shogun—the highest political position in feudal Japan—his vision of a unified nation continued to shape the archipelago's destiny long after his death. At the time of his assassination, Nobunaga had already forced the last Ashikaga shogun into exile and functioned as the de facto ruler of central Japan, controlling vital trade routes, the capital region, and major economic centers that formed the beating heart of Japanese commerce and culture.

The work of unification that Nobunaga had begun with such revolutionary fervor would be completed by his successors, Hideyoshi and later Tokugawa Ieyasu. These men inherited not just territories and armies, but a transformative vision: the idea that Japan could be more than a collection of warring provinces, that it could become a unified nation capable of controlling its own destiny. In this sense, Nobunaga's death at Honnō-ji represented not an ending, but a metamorphosis—the violent birth of modern Japan from the ashes of feudal chaos.

Yet among all the documented consequences of that fateful night, perhaps none is more intriguing than the fate of Yasuke, the African warrior who had risen from slavery to become one of Japan's most enigmatic samurai. Historical records, sparse as they are regarding this remarkable figure, suggest that after Nobunaga's death, Yasuke fought desperately to protect the heir, Nobutada, at Nijō Castle. When that final battle was lost and Nobutada chose the honorable path of seppuku, Yasuke was captured by Akechi's forces.

According to surviving accounts, Akechi Mitsuhide—the same man who had harbored such hatred for the foreign samurai—chose not to execute Yasuke. Instead, in a final act of contempt, he allegedly declared that the African was "an animal and not a true Japanese," and therefore unworthy of death by a samurai's blade. This dismissal, intended as the ultimate insult, may have inadvertently saved Yasuke's life.

What happened next remains one of history's most tantalizing mysteries. Yasuke simply vanished from all historical records, disappearing as completely as if he had never existed. No documentation survives to chronicle his movements, his fate, or his final resting place. Some scholars theorize he was sold back into slavery and shipped to European ports; others suggest he may have found refuge among Japan's Christian communities or escaped to the mainland. A few romantic historians have even proposed that he lived out his days in peaceful anonymity, perhaps as a farmer or craftsman in some remote village where his extraordinary past would never be discovered.

The truth, however, may be far stranger than any academic theory could encompass. For in the realm where legend meets history, where documented fact gives way to whispered myth, the story of Yasuke transcends the limitations of mere historical record. Perhaps his disappearance was not an ending at all, but a transformation—a passage from the world of mortal men into something far more enduring and mysterious.

The Nijō Castle that stands today in Kyoto, built by Tokugawa Ieyasu in 1603, occupies the same ground where these momentous events unfolded, though none of the original structures remain. Visitors who walk through its elegant halls and perfectly manicured gardens rarely realize they are treading on soil that once witnessed the final acts of one of history's most remarkable lives.

In the end, Yasuke's legacy rests not in stone monuments or written chronicles, but in the simple yet revolutionary truth that honor, courage, and nobility of spirit recognize no boundaries of race, nation, or birth. He proved that a man's worth is measured not by the circumstances of his origin, but by the choices he makes when tested by fate and adversity.

And perhaps, in the realm beyond history's reach, his story continues still—waiting for the moment when the world has need of legends once more.

ABOUT THE AUTHOR

Braxton A. Cosby is a multi-award-winning author and dreamer with a passion for inspiring others to love, in spite of circumstance and convenience. As CEO of Cosby Media Productions and Starchild Comics, he pursues his calling to pen young adult, sci-fi, and fantasy novels that are smart, witty, and thought-provoking—all with unmatched vigor and dedication to solid storytelling. Braxton has written over 20 novels, 5 screenplays, and 8 comic scripts. He lives in Atlanta, Georgia, with his wife and four children.

FOLLOW Braxton @:

Instagram:
@braxtonacosby
Twitter:
@BraxtonACosby
Facebook:
https://www.facebook.com/BraxtonACosby

Websites:
www.braxtoncosby.com
www.theredgeminichronicles
www.cosbymediaproductions.com

OTHER OFFERINGS FROM THE YASUKE STORY

GRAPHIC NOVEL

YASUKE: RESURRECTION

BOOK II

COMIC

BLOOD MOONS: A YASUKE STORY

www.cosbymediaproductions.com

www.ingramcontent.com/pod-product-compliance
Lightning Source LLC
LaVergne TN
LVHW050623100826
845148LV00011B/1702

* 9 7 9 8 8 9 9 6 5 0 7 8 9 *